Coo

KAELA NOEL

ILLUSTRATIONS BY
Celia Krampien

GREENWILLOW BOOKS
An Imprint of HarperCollins*Publishers*

Coo

Text copyright © 2020 by Kaela Noel

Illustrations copyright © 2020 by Celia Krampien

The text of this book is set in 13-point Sabon MT.
Book design by Paul Zakris

Library of Congress Cataloging-in-Publication Data

Names: Noel, Kaela, author.
Title: Coo / by Kaela Noel.
Description: First edition. | New York :
Greenwillow Books, an Imprint of HarperCollins Publishers, [2020] |
Audience: Ages 8–12. | Audience: Grades 4–6. |
Summary: "Coo, a ten-year-old girl raised by a flock of pigeons, delights in finally making human contact, but quickly learns that our world is more cruel and complicated than she could have guessed"— Provided by publisher.
Identifiers: LCCN 2019041823 |
ISBN 9780062955975 (hardcover) | ISBN 9780062955999 (epub)
Subjects: CYAC: Human-animal relationships—Fiction. | Pigeons—Fiction. |
Abandoned children—Fiction. | City and town life—Fiction.
Classification: LCC PZ7.1.N628 Coo 2020 | DDC [Fic]—dc23
LC record available at https://lccn.loc.gov/2019041823

20 21 22 23 24 PC/LSCH 10 9 8 7 6 5 4 3 2 1
First Edition

Greenwillow Books

For
Alice Peach

Contents

Once Upon a Time

April breezes, warm and mild as clean laundry, fluttered across the dark rail yard.

The trains rested on their hushed tracks. In an hour dawn would break and the Monday-morning commute would begin.

For now no people were about, not even the workers in big helmets and neon vests who tended the yard overnight.

The pigeons who lived on the roof of the

abandoned factory beside the yard were deep in slumber, too.

All but one.

A charcoal-dark yearling with a white stripe across his wings couldn't sleep. Instead he roamed around the alley that ran next to the factory, peering up at the small hut that glowed there.

Sometimes things came flying from the hut's windows. Candy bar wrappers, banana peels, old newspapers.

And food.

Inside, the night watchman munched on a strawberry glazed from Donut Time, the shop around the corner. On the tiny television screen perched on his desk, a weather reporter pointed to green and red radar clouds of rain on their way to the city. Reception was terrible, and the picture kept going gray. The donut was stale. Teetering atop the TV, the watchman's coffee maker hissed and dripped.

Hardly anyone came into the factory yard

through the back alley. Most nights the guard dozed, only sputtering awake when his walkie-talkie crackled with chatter from the rail yard crews. The messages were never for him.

The weather report ended and a news segment about the dangers of sugar began.

The guard stopped chewing to look down at his belly.

He slid open the tiny window over his shoulder and tossed the strawberry donut into the darkness. Eyes tugging shut, he sighed, and soon even the coffee pot's beep as it finished brewing wasn't enough to wake him.

The pigeon with the bright white stripe was still nibbling the pink donut when a young woman holding a small, tightly wrapped bundle came to stand at the bend where the alley led out to the street.

He paused, a crumb of glaze in his beak. One of the first things a pigeon learned was how to act around humans. When one came near, you scuttled away, unless it had food. Even then, you kept your distance. Humans were unpredictable.

Like this one.

He watched as she tiptoed closer, walking far more softly than humans usually did, and placed the bundle on the step of the watchman's hut. She exhaled a sharp breath. Then she briskly disappeared the way she had come, melting into the deep shadows.

Cautiously, the pigeon stepped over to the bundle. It was larger than a loaf of bread and wrapped up in cloth. He had never seen anything like it left in the alley before.

Hopping up on the bundle, he looked in.

He flapped back in shock.

A tiny human lay in the blankets. Drowsily she waved her little fists. One nearly knocked the pigeon over, but he dodged it and came closer. The baby's eyes were squeezed shut and her nose wiggled.

The pigeon knew for sure that big humans never left tiny humans alone. All squabs needed care. Something was very wrong.

Nestled in her warm bundle, calm in the early morning shadows, the baby blinked open her eyes. Above her was the purplish morning sky. Her eyes were too new to focus on the faint stars scattered in their spring constellations. A train screeched lightly in the distance and she flinched. But she didn't cry. She flexed her plump fingers and waited.

While the guard dozed in ignorance, and her mother's footsteps faded into silence, one of the strangest, most miraculous, most uncanny events in city history unfolded in the little alley beside the rail yard.

The pigeon stared into the face of the baby. The baby stared back at the pigeon.

The pigeon zoomed up to the dovecote on the roof where his flock slept and woke them.

Not everyone thought his plan was a good one, but some of them were curious enough to skim down to see what he meant. An abandoned human squab—strange indeed.

As a dozen birds scrutinized her, the baby's eyes widened. Then she smiled.

"Rain soon," said Burr, the pigeon with the white-striped wing. He could smell it in the air. "Needs shelter, squab."

"True," a burly pigeon named Hoop said. "Bad for squabs, rain."

"Lift squab up, us," Burr said. "Take her to dovecote, us."

The others hesitated.

"Right, Burr is," said Pim, a very old bird. "Needs care. Hurry."

While the baby turned her small head every which way to look, twelve pigeons nicked their beaks into her bundle. Some grasped her wool shawl; others the soft pink blanket sandwiched beneath; two or three managed to hook into the cotton romper she wore snugly snapped against her body.

The pigeons began to flap their wings, soothing as a swaying cradle.

Faster and faster they flapped. Loose feathers spiraled into the darkness. They flapped still harder.

A warm breeze tumbled down the alley, tickling the weeds as it went. When it reached the birds, it pushed under their wings.

The baby's swaddling tight in their beaks, the wind whistling through their feathers, the pigeons lifted off.

In his hut, the dozing night watchman stirred. What was that rustling? He stood up, scattering donut crumbs from his lap and knocking an empty coffee mug to the floor.

Outside, the pigeons startled at the noise. One lost grip of the shawl in his beak, and the bundle shuddered.

Burr flapped his wings faster. Never had he flown so hard.

The birds recovered. Hoisting the bundle in spurts and staggers, they heaved above the watchman's hut, over the chain-link fence, up and up and up.

The pigeons steered a few feet to the left and landed on the roof outside the doorway of their cozy dovecote.

The baby opened her eyes and looked around at her new home.

Chapter One
Roof

Every day for Coo and her flock began the same. Even the day when everything changed.

Coo woke when the sun rose, crawled from her nest of newspaper on the dovecote's floor into the brightness of the roof, and looked over her collection of plastic bags. She liked to put on a new outfit in the morning, something the pigeons didn't understand at all. Her hands brushed against a red bag she loved and she sighed. Like many of the others, it was painfully small now. Instead, she stuck her feet into the holes she'd ripped in the bottom of a large yellow bag, shimmied her arms through the handles, and padded it out with some newspaper.

Freshly dressed, she picked over the pigeons' morning haul of dumpster food for the least-smashed donut and settled down to nibble her breakfast while she watched the trains slide along their tracks in the ragged brown field below. Beyond, hazy in the distance, were trees and fences and a hodgepodge of big and small buildings packed together. She watched the tiny figures of other birds, ones she didn't know, glide in the sun between the jumbled rooftops.

The air was cold and smelled clean, like autumn. A frigid rain had fallen overnight. She wiggled her chilly toes and added more newspaper into her plastic-bag booties. It was getting to be the time of year when it would take even more layers of padding to stay warm. Hoop and Ka had already started foraging for the newsprint she'd need and grabbing extra bags for her whenever they found them. Small piles were growing in the back of Coo's nest, the bags sorted carefully by color, but she needed more of both to get through the winter.

She wanted more newspapers for other reasons, too. For years she'd liked looking at the pictures in them, but now Coo pored over them with an interest that felt like hunger, even though she had long ago learned you couldn't eat paper. She liked looking at pictures of faces—human faces. She collected her favorites and kept them far in the back of the dovecote, safe from the wind and rain.

From inside her romper she pulled out the clump of papers Ka had dragged up for her that morning. Mostly the paper was covered with gray scratch marks, but there was one big black-and-white picture in the middle. Coo stuffed more donut in her mouth, then smoothed the paper out.

A face. Not a pigeon face. A human face. Eyes,

nose, ears. The face was making a frown, and Coo copied it, feeling her lips turn down.

"Human," she said, and pointed to it. "See, Burr?" Coo spoke the pigeon's language—the only language she knew.

Burr perched on her knee, pecking at fallen crumbs. He was an old, slim bird the color of the roof when it was wet, with a bright white stripe across his wings. The stripe was beautiful but also dangerous. It made him easy for hawks to spot. Not that Coo really worried about it. Hawks never hunted pigeons when she was nearby.

"Doing what, human?" Coo asked.

Burr didn't know. The pigeons never knew much about the pictures in the paper. Coo felt a pang. That feeling of hunger returned. It was not in her stomach. It came from somewhere else, somewhere much harder to understand.

The flock was milling about the roof. New Tiktik, a bright-eyed yearling, was cleaning her speckled gray feathers in the crisp, rain-scrubbed sunshine. Ever-grumpy Roohoo hunched in a ball of purplish-red feathers on the roof ledge nearby. As usual, he was unpigeonishly alone.

Other pigeons swooped overhead and pecked the weeds around the dovecote doorway. Old Tiktik, one of the oldest in the flock besides Burr, sipped water from a puddle.

Coo dropped the paper and went to stare into the puddle. Round, broad, and bare, and ringed with matted yellow-brown hair. Big eyes. No feathers at all. She opened her mouth and so did the rippling picture in the water. A big dark O.

Coo looked up from the puddle and over the roof edge. A human dressed in neon orange was walking along the crisscrossing tracks. For years Coo had hidden when she saw humans down below, but recently she'd become more curious— and brave.

She leaned over the raised ledge of the roof and studied the shape of its face. Yes, it was definitely like the faces on the newsprint, and the face she saw when she looked into puddles. Her face. She popped the last chunk of donut into her mouth and ran her sticky fingers over her nose and lips and cheeks.

Although she'd almost always known she was not like the birds, for years she didn't care.

Not anymore. Now she wondered and worried about the ways she was different.

Her family had feathers; she had skin and hair. They had hard beaks; she had a soft nose. They could fly; she could jump and walk, but no matter how much she flapped her arms, so far they'd never lifted her from the ground for more than a moment.

The loneliest feeling in the world was watching the flock take off and being left behind all alone on the roof. Coo longed to fly.

Coo often asked Burr why she couldn't. But *why* wasn't something that interested her flock much. Coo wondered about *why* all the time. She asked again, and Burr answered as he always did.

"Human, you. Like the healer." Burr meant the plump human who plodded down the alley most afternoons to scatter seed and bread for the flock, and who also, mysteriously, sometimes scooped up sick birds and returned them many days later, all well.

"Can't fly, humans? Ever? Why?" Coo asked, even though she knew he didn't know.

Burr couldn't answer every one of Coo's questions, but he could travel all over the world beyond the roof without getting lost, live through winter in just his feathers without ever getting cold, and forage grub all year long. Coo couldn't do any of that. She relied on the pigeons to bring her food to eat. She'd never been down from the roof since she was an infant, not once, though she had attempted it, in fits and starts, a few times. The truth was she was afraid of the ground. The very thought of walking around in the world she peered down upon, the one the birds flew over effortlessly, made her shiver.

If only she could fly.

It came up every so often. Mostly only the younger pigeons who didn't know better mentioned it, especially the curious ones like New Tiktik.

"Fly yet, you?" New Tiktik asked over and over when she was still a newly feathered squab, not noticing how it made Coo turn warm and blush. Blushing—feeling embarrassed—was a human thing.

"Never fly, her," huffed Roohoo the last time New Tiktik had asked. "Look—no wings. No feathers. Not a bird! Flying? Humans? Never! Kick pigeons, them. Watch out, all. Kick, Coo. Ouch!"

Coo had glowered at that but said nothing. She would never kick a pigeon and Roohoo knew it, but it was best not to argue with him. He was the cleverest bird in the flock, and the most stubborn. It was impossible to win an argument with him.

Scooping Burr onto her shoulder, Coo wandered

away from the roof's edge, and from the puddle and its puzzles.

The roof was a broad and bumpy square. It was Coo's whole world. Once, long ago, before her time with the flock, someone had painted it silver, but most of the silver had since flaked off, revealing grayish-black tar beneath. In the cracks of the tar grew plants that rose green and leggy each spring, bloomed in many colors in the summer, and then turned brown and died each fall.

One side of the building ran along a street, beyond which was an abandoned lot dense with weeds. Cars—those big, pigeon-squashing monsters, only spoken of in hushed tones—seldom traveled it, but Coo avoided that side of the roof anyway, sticking to the two sides that bordered the rail yard and the one that ran along the alley.

On that side sat the most important part of Coo's home.

The dovecote.

It was a round, stout little building a bit taller

than Coo herself and wide enough for her to lay down inside. It had a small open doorway and a pitched roof, and was packed with shelves of nesting boxes for the flock and a many-layered floor of feathers and newspaper for Coo. Its whitish-gray paint was flaking and streaked brown with age.

Coo never really thought about where the dovecote had come from any more than she thought about the roof itself or the other things on it. Long before her time, some human had built it. The flock had a dim knowledge of this: a human who made pigeons race one another, and fed them, and then disappeared. But that was many years ago, a dozen or more murky generations of pigeon memories. The flock had long since turned wild.

That morning Coo padded across the roof, passing what had been her favorite clump of summer wildflowers, their bright pink blooms now drooping gray. She sat in the slight shadow their stalks made. Here was her collection of pebbles, sticks, and piles of leaves, carefully arranged in groups. She was playing a long-running game of Find Food with whatever pigeons she could snag for her pretend flights. She dashed back and forth flapping her arms like wings, looking for pretend bagels, donuts, and fruit under the cracked red plastic chair that sat by the dovecote. Pigeons didn't play that way on their own, and their confusion always slowed down the game.

She was scooping up pretend donuts that were really rocks and handing them to Burr—Burr was always patient about standing where she told him and doing what she said, even if he never really understood the point—when Roohoo appeared.

"No sense, you." He landed next to a brownish speckled leaf that was really a pretend banana.

Coo had long since stopped trying to rope Roohoo into her games, but he still watched, carefully observing so he could criticize her.

"No sense, no skills," he sniffed.

"Not true," said Burr. "Hush, Roohoo. Coo helps. Has skills, her. Know this, you."

These were Coo's skills: her thin, wiggly fingers plucked gum from feathers and glass shards from toes. She chased eggs that rolled from nests and put them back so they would hatch, and rescued the squabs who tried to fly too soon and fell squeaking onto the floor of the dovecote. With her sharp nails she quickly tore open the plastic sacks of bread the pigeons had learned to fetch, two birds to a bag, and heave back to the roof. She could even stuff leaves and bits of newspaper into holes and cracks to fix the leaks that sprung in the roof of the dovecote. She kept the roof and dovecote tidy, too, cleaning up the newsprint full of pigeon droppings and the plastic bags she used for the toilet.

Best of all, Coo could scare hawks.

Before Coo, the roof had been to the hawks what the dumpster was to the pigeons. There was no tastier snack to a hawk than a plump, trash-fattened pigeon. The hawks had grazed on the roof regularly, coasting slow and silent overhead while Coo's flock huddled in shivering terror inside the dovecote. But since she'd grown large enough to run and screech, no hawk had bothered the flock. Nothing made Coo prouder than that.

"Smart, me," Coo muttered to Roohoo. She plopped down beside a pile of teeny-tiny gray pebbles that were pretend bagels. "Scare hawks, me."

"So far," said Roohoo.

Coo ignored him, and he swooped up into the air and went back to the dovecote.

Chapter Two
Hawk

Coo was sorting three pretend pink donuts and was just starting to get tired of playing when the warning cry went up from the flock. Coo leaped to her feet and scanned the sky.

There it was. Broad wings speckled brown and white, a fan of red tail feathers, flying quicker than a piece of litter in the wind: a hawk.

Coo stood up and yelped.

Burr fluttered toward the dovecote, joining the

pigeons who raced into the doorway from every direction.

The hawk was right behind.

"Away!" Coo ran across the roof with her arms spread wide. It was harder to run when it got colder. The plastic-bag booties she wore on her feet were slippery, even on the rough surface of the roof. "Go, hawk!"

Her yell always made hawks arc away into the wide blue sky.

Almost always.

This hawk was very hungry. Ignoring her, it dove into the panicked stream of pigeons funneling toward the dovecote door. The pigeons scattered, and the hawk appeared with a captive flailing between its talons. A bird as dark gray as a summer rain cloud with a white stripe across its wings.

Burr!

"No!" Coo zoomed toward Burr. The wind roared in her ears, and a sudden gust pushed itself behind her and across the roof. Glossy brown feathers rippling, the hawk braced against it, unable to swoop up through the wall of air.

Coo punched it square in the chest. Its claws opened, and Burr thudded to the roof.

"Go!" Coo screamed at the hawk. "Go!"

The hawk's sharp, small, smart eyes met Coo's. The wind shifted. The hawk screeched once and took off.

"Gone, hawk!" Coo leaped in the air and for a moment felt the wind tickle against the plastic soles of her feet—an almost-flying feeling.

But her triumph fizzed out like air from one of the miraculous balloons that sometimes snagged on the roof.

Burr lay where the hawk had dropped him, and he wasn't moving.

Coo fell to her knees and bundled Burr into her arms. He gasped in shallow, rapid bursts. "Hurt, you?" Coo's heart rocked against her ribs. Other pigeons had been injured like this, or worse, but not one she loved like Burr. Not Burr. "Speak, you! Speak!"

Burr bleated faintly. "Left wing. Broken, maybe."

"Be still, you," Coo said, trying hard to stop shaking. "Help you, me? How?"

Burr was silent, breathing heavily, but New Tiktik landed on Coo's shoulder and said, "The healer. Ground. Bring Burr, you."

All those lucky birds the healer fixed in the past had been injured on the ground. The healer clucked in a way that made no sense, bundled the wounded ones into a box she carried, and took them away. Days chilled and warmed, moons shrank and grew. Coo inched taller and needed bigger plastic bags to wear. Time passed, but often the hurt birds returned to the flock, all better.

Like Hoop. When Coo had been much smaller, Hoop had snagged her foot on the alley's fence, cutting it so badly she could not walk. But the healer found her and took her away. One day

Hoop came back and her foot was just like new. How did the healer do it?

Coo had asked Hoop many times *how* she'd been healed, and *where* she had been while she was away, but her explanations were hopelessly vague. There wasn't time to pester Hoop again for answers.

"Up here, us," Coo said to New Tiktik. "Down there, healer. Me? Always up here."

"No." Burr's whole body shuddered as he spoke. "Long ago. Small you. Remember?"

Coo shivered. The one part of her own story she didn't like remembering was the very beginning, the time when she'd been down on the ground, away from the safety of the roof and the flock, before the pigeons had rescued her.

"Go down now, you," New Tiktik said.

"How?" Coo asked. "How now? Can't fly, me. Down, how?"

But Coo already knew how. Clinging to the side of the building was a strange stack of thin metal slats that zigzagged all the way to the ground. A fire escape. Over the years, driven by hunger and curiosity, Coo had lowered herself onto it a few times and even shimmied down some of the stairs. Each time, the slats had shook under her feet like winter-brittle twigs and spooked her into scrambling back onto the roof's solid ground.

She had long ago decided that the roof was home, her whole world, and since she couldn't fly, everything beyond it was unnecessary.

Almost.

She looked at Burr and his sickeningly bent wing.

Pigeons injured on the roof never got better. Their feathers turned dull and their skin loosened against their bones, even as Coo fed them and kept them warm. The other pigeons in the flock avoided them as they got weaker and weaker, nudging sick ones from the flock as pigeons did, until it was only Coo who paid attention. She nursed them day and night. But the first cold snap always sucked the breath from their beaks and they died. It had happened to Mop, to Pip, to Tiwoo.

Pigeons didn't think of one another as particularly special—the flock mattered more than any of its individual members—but Coo did. She couldn't help it. And Burr was most special of all. Coo sat on her knees in the dovecote doorway, rocking him in her arms. He was the one who had found her, who had recognized her and brought her to her family.

"Okay, me," whispered Burr. "Don't worry, you."

"Hush," Coo muttered back. "Help you, me. Somehow."

She tucked Burr into the darkest, safest part of the dovecote, forcing herself to ignore how some of the others were already inching away from him, and then went to look at the fire escape.

"Go on, you. Don't need wings."

It was New Tiktik. She was a little bit different from the others, like Burr. She made two quick swooping loops around Coo and settled on her shoulder.

"Scary," Coo whispered.

"Scared, you? Why? Chase hawks, you! Not scary."

"Chased bad today, me."

The ground loomed far below, as far away as a future where Burr survived. But Coo had to get there. Somehow.

"Go on, you," New Tiktik said. "Try."

Coo went back to the dovecote and found Burr. His breathing was raspy and shallow.

"P-pain." The old bird shivered. "Much pain now."

The other pigeons looked on, curious but distant, as Coo found a clean plastic bag and a pile of leaves and made a soft pouch for Burr. Hands trembling, she tucked him in and tied the bag snugly around her chest.

"Down to the ground, me."

The flock murmured in surprise.

"How?" asked Hoop.

Coo pointed with a shaky finger to the fire escape. Only the warm softness of Burr against her chest calmed her as she tiptoed to the edge. The rest of the flock followed, hovering around her, curious.

"Belongs on the ground, her," said Roohoo. "Human, she is. Hurry up, Coo."

Coo ignored him and dangled both legs over the roof's ledge.

"Dangerous, this." Old Tiktik bobbed toward her. "Ground? Coo? No. Can't fly, you."

"Climb down, me," Coo said, though the word *climb* was an awkward one in pigeon. Birds did not climb anywhere, up or down. Coo had no word for what she meant to describe. She said something closer to "hop a lot" and hoped it made sense.

"Wait." Panting, Burr pushed his head out of the pouch. "Right, Old Tiktik. Dangerous, Coo.

Stay with flock, you. Part of life, dying." He took a deep breath. "Not worth it, me."

"No!" gasped Coo.

How could Burr think he wasn't worth saving?

"Flock is safest," said Hem. "No wings, you. Stay up here."

"Stay up here, me?" said Coo. "Hurt, Burr. Die, him!"

"Nimble, Coo!" said New Tiktik. "Safe, her. Go down, Coo."

Coo felt like she did when she spun in circles too many times. Dizzy. But New Tiktik's confidence gave her a burst of courage. And Burr didn't know what he was talking about. She was sure of that. The pain was making him confused.

She stretched and stretched her right leg until her toes brushed the slats of the fire escape. She inched her right foot down. She swung her left foot down beside it.

The whole sky was at her back. For a moment, the shiver she felt was excitement. She'd spent every day and night of all the seasons she'd ever known in one small, flat place, wondering more and more about what was beyond. Especially about the others, the ones who looked like her—the humans. The shiver came back, fiercer now. Her fear festered like a moldy bagel in the pit of her stomach, but seeping around that feeling was curiosity.

She began to inch along the fire escape, slat by slat, scooting down on her behind. The rusty metal was very cold through the thin plastic of her romper. One flight down, she ripped the slippery plastic bags off her feet and let them drift away. The metal was frigid, but she felt more stable. At the landing she shut her eyes and stopped.

"Keep going, you!" said New Tiktik, swooping around her.

Other flock members floated down, too, hopping from rail to rail, watching. She didn't dare look into the pouch at Burr. One more word from him about dying and Coo thought she would crumble right off the side.

"Rescue you again, we can't," grumbled Roohoo when she paused for a very long time, covering her face with her hands. "Too big now, you. Keep moving! Scared, you?"

"No," Coo spat in Roohoo's direction. "Not scared, me."

For the next few minutes, she forced herself to look at the side of the building a foot or two away. All the way down were chilly holes, damp and dark as nighttime. Some were covered in warped planks and others in smooth, solid planes of what looked like ice, while others were open to the air.

"Windows," Roohoo said, plopping down next to her as she stared. "Trick birds, them. Smash! Hurt!"

Coo didn't like to think of birds crashing into windows. She peered into them and then inched on, full of wonder. How had she never thought about what was below the roof, what she couldn't see? How had she never thought about what was inside the other buildings nearby? Was there food inside them? Other people? The pigeons never talked about what was inside things, or under them. Even at her hungriest times, Coo had never stopped to think, either. Now she was startled.

She reached the last flight of stairs, and when she dared to look down, the gray ribbon on the ground below had transformed into a splatter of individual stones. The green-brown fuzz of the shrubs was now sticks and leaves that looked just like the plants that grew on the roof. Surprised, Coo paused. But of course the ground looked different as you got nearer to it, just as a pigeon grew bigger and more detailed as it flew closer to you.

Coo teetered on the last landing. The stairs became, confusingly, a rack of metal bars that didn't reach all the way to the ground. Coo puzzled over this for a long time.

"Hurry, you," said New Tiktik. "Here soon, healer."

Coo swung her body over the side. The ladder lurched. Coo held on as it screeched downward, finally coming to a stop a few feet above the ground. She took a deep breath and jumped.

She landed with a hard bounce on a thicket of weeds and twigs, staggered once, and caught her balance. Then she crouched and looked around.

The side of Coo's building rose high above. From the roof the fence was just a thin gray line, but now it was a barrier that reached terrifyingly far over her head. Coo tilted her head back until her neck pinched, but she still couldn't take everything in. Her heart began to pound. Beyond the impossibly high fence was an area covered in small rocks, and beyond that, the other building. The sky was just a scrap of blue between the two brick walls. It was the tiniest sky she'd ever seen.

Looking at it, she felt like throwing up.

"Ground's different, huh?" New Tiktik circled Coo in excited laps.

Coo couldn't find her voice to reply. With every bone in her body, all she wanted was to bolt back up the fire escape to home.

Chapter Three
Ground

Coo did not try to climb back up the fire escape. Instead, she opened the plastic-bag pouch on her chest and peered in at Burr.

"Pain," he said. "Bag too tight."

Coo untied his pouch and placed it on the ground. She fluffed the shredded newspaper. "Better?"

Burr stretched his neck and whimpered. "Ground. Danger. Be careful, you. Not safe here."

"Fine, me. Stop worrying, you."

Peering through the fence, Coo saw the hut. It was much bigger than she expected, taller and wider than the dovecote. She knew from the birds that long ago, humans spent hours every day sitting inside of it.

No human had come to or gone from the hut since she'd been big enough to lean over the roof's ledge and watch the alley. The hut was boarded up and covered in brown vines. She could hear the big metal trains singing over their tracks nearby, but for the first time ever, she couldn't see them. They were hidden by a tall, solid wall behind the hut.

Maybe, Coo thought, she should go looking for the healer. First she had to find a way through the chain-link fence that ran between the alley and the factory. She glanced at Burr hidden inside his plastic-bag pouch. Then she took a few cautious steps into the underbrush.

A shredded yellow plastic bag, matching the

one she wore, shimmied in the wind where it was caught on the fence. Leaves crackled under her feet along with strange things she never saw on the roof, like a pile of glinting ice pieces that somehow weren't melted.

"Glass," said New Tiktik. "Ouch! Careful. Cuts you."

Coo was startled. New Tiktik was right—it was glass, just like the slivers she picked from the feet of injured birds. She had never imagined so much of it in one place before. She carefully stepped around it.

Coo heard a wisp of noise behind her. New Tiktik and the other pigeons fled upward in a single beat of wings. Coo whipped around.

A fat, hairy, gray thing slinked along the ground toward Burr. Big white teeth were bared against its pink gums.

Coo had never seen a cat before, but she'd heard plenty of stories.

She jumped over the mess of weeds between her and Burr and shrieked. The cat froze. It yowled at Coo. Then it shot through a hole in the fence and disappeared.

"Hurt more?" Coo said, scooping Burr into her arms. "Oh, Burr. Scary, scary! Sorry, me."

"Not hurt more, me," Burr said in a frighteningly quiet voice. "Hurt, you?"

"No," said Coo. "Big, me. Bigger than cat, me."

"Too dangerous here," Burr murmured. "Go back up, you. Not worth this, me."

"No! Wait, me. Help you, me."

The other pigeons still circled in alarm above, but Roohoo landed with a thump on the fence above her.

"Dangerous, see?" he said. "Ground's no place for pigeons. Come from here, you."

The world beyond the roof was frightening in ways Coo had never imagined. But it was also the only place that could save Burr—whether he thought he was worth saving, or not.

She nestled him against her chest and crouched in the bushes to wait.

The sun was high above the alley when the healer at last arrived. A fringe of feathery gray peeped from beneath the poofy red mound on her head. A ragged brown layer of fuzz circled her neck. Her face was very round and her skin much more wrinkled than Coo's own. She made a peculiar whistling sound as she crunched down the gravel.

"Oh, my dear feathered friends, here I come," she chanted, swinging a cloth sack in one hand. "It's a bright autumn day and I'm here to say, come have some lunch!"

At the sound of the human's voice, the flock quit circling and zoomed to the ground. The healer began to scatter birdseed in big fistfuls from the sack.

Half-hidden behind the bushes, Coo stared in shock. The healer was far taller than Coo thought humans were. Taller than Coo for sure. And wider. Roohoo and the others had lied, it seemed. Or didn't know what they were talking about at all. How was Coo supposed to be the same thing as that?

Yet, as Coo watched and listened, the healer's face rippled through different expressions, just like Coo's did when she looked at herself in puddles. Maybe humans came in more than one size and shape, like birds.

All at once Coo realized faces, not flying, were the way humans and pigeons were most different. Pigeon faces never changed, no matter how they were talking or feeling.

Coo stood up. Her feet had become as heavy as rain-soaked bagels.

New Tiktik broke off from the other pigeons, most of whom had lost interest in Burr and Coo as soon as the seed was thrown, and landed beside Coo.

"Speak, you," she nudged. "Go on, you."

"Scared, me. Bad human, maybe."

"No. Good human. Heals us, remember?"

That was true. Coo thought of Hoop.

Burr cooed faintly in the bag.

"Help you, me," Coo whispered.

Coo crawled along the fence until she found the rip where the cat had escaped. Taking a deep breath, sheltering Burr with both her hands, she climbed through.

It took a moment for the healer to notice Coo where she stood a few feet away, holding out the slightly stirring bundle that was Burr.

"Whoa! Startled me, dear," the healer said, jumping back. "Who are you? What are you doing here all by yourself?"

Even though the others had told Coo many times that humans couldn't speak pigeon, Coo had never really believed them. But maybe they were right. Trying to make sense of what the healer said was impossible, worse than listening to a chattering sparrow. Thinking of sparrows distracted Coo for a moment from her flip-flopping nerves. She took a step closer and, trembling, pushed Burr forward.

"Hurt, him," Coo said as clearly and slowly as she could. "Broken wing."

"What was that, dear? Are you wearing—is that a plastic bag? My goodness. Where are your parents?"

Even sparrows could sound out a few words of pigeon, though their pronunciation was always very silly. Not this human. Her speech was just squab babble.

"Hurt. Broken. Wing." This time Coo unwrapped Burr's pouch.

The healer scooped Burr from Coo's hands and peered at him with large, watery blue eyes.

"A pigeon. Poor thing. I can help. I've helped others from this flock. But never mind the bird; we need to get *you* help. Right away."

Still holding Burr, the healer stooped down. Her eyes squinted.

Coo scrambled back.

"Your hair is so matted! There's dirt all over

your face. You're barefoot! When was the last time you took a bath? Or ate a decent meal? You're thinner than a string bean, sweetheart. Where are your parents?"

"Help him, you?" asked Coo.

The healer frowned. "Do you speak English?"

Coo stared.

"Can't talk, healer," she said to New Tiktik as the bird zipped past. "Why not?"

"No humans talk pigeon. Only you, Coo."

"Why?"

"Just can't," said New Tiktik. "Not smart like birds, humans. Very sad, it is."

Coo gazed at the healer. She kept speaking gibberish.

"I can't understand you, but maybe you understand me. What's your name, dear? Let's start there, at least. Name? My name is Bettina Tully, but everyone calls me Tully."

The human pointed at herself and said, very slowly, "Tully. TULLY. Tul-lee."

Maybe humans just had their own speech, like sparrows, and crows, and seagulls.

"Tul-lee," echoed Coo, finally.

"Yes! That's my name. I am Tully. But who are *you*?"

Slowly, Coo pointed at herself and clucked the name the pigeons had always called her. "Khooo." Long, soft, and fluttery, the sound came from a place deep in her throat.

"Coo," Tully said.

"Khooo," Coo said again.

"Coo," Tully said, with a harder *c* sound and only the slightest breathy *hoo* in the *oo*. Coo felt a bit sorry for the healer. Not to be able to speak! It was horrible to think about.

"Well, nice to meet you, Coo." Tully frowned. "You're in such rough shape. I'd call for help right now, but my cell phone is charging at home."

As she babbled, Tully pulled a box with holes from her bag and shifted Burr into its dark, open mouth.

Coo's heart panged watching him disappear. She hadn't thought about this part, not at all.

"There," said Tully, closing the small metal flap on the box. "The pigeon is nice and safe now. I'll see what I can do for him."

Coo stared at the box holding Burr and tried to decide whether to rip it away from the healer.

"Would you come with me?" Tully reached out her hand. "We'll go somewhere you can get help."

Coo scooted backward.

"I promise I won't bite. Are you hungry?" Tully pulled a brown paper sack from her scruffy tote and opened it. "I was saving these for later, but perhaps you would like them. A reward for caring so much for a hurt bird."

Coo looked at the healer in shock. She was holding a donut. A perfect, round donut with pink sprinkles! Donuts usually arrived on the roof mashed, mangled, and stale. A perfect donut was a miracle.

 In one swift dart, Coo snatched the beautiful donut from Tully's hand. She scurried back and began to devour it.

"You're famished," murmured Tully. "Oh dear. I have a sandwich, too. It was my lunch, but you should eat it."

Coo peered at the bag Tully handed her. Inside were plain bread slices and between them gloopy green shapes and even sludgier light brown mud. Mixed with all that muck, smashed between the perfect bread, was a bunch of weeds.

"Avocado, hummus, and sprouts," Tully said. "A health food sandwich."

Did humans really eat mud and weeds?

Coo hesitated. Her stomach rumbled again. She could nibble the bread at least, and hopefully wipe off the dirt and whatever the rancid green stuff was. She'd long ago learned to tell when food had spoiled, and she didn't want to get sick. The weeds would be easy to spit out, too. She'd eaten plenty of bagels that had spent time in puddles. This wasn't much different.

She took a small bite and swallowed in shock. It *was* different. The bread was normal bread, but the mud was not like any kind of dirt she knew—it was wonderful. So was the green muck. Smooth, salty, a little sweet. Not at all rotten. The weeds were strange, but tender, not tough like the ones on the roof.

Coo could have eaten ten more sandwiches. She peered at Tully.

"I can see food is the way to gain your trust," Tully said. "How about warmth? Here, take this. You look so cold."

Tully removed the red top of her head and the layer of brown feathers around her neck. Underneath were gray hair and bare skin.

"I knitted these. I hope they aren't too big."

Tully pushed the fluffy things toward Coo, who stared at them.

"Here. I'll help you."

Coo froze as Tully plopped the red fuzz onto her head, then wrapped the strange strand of brown feathers around Coo's neck. Suddenly everything felt warmer.

"There. Hats and scarves always help."

Coo had never been so close to someone who wasn't a bird, nor had she ever felt anything so soft against her skin as the hat and scarf. Not even new feathers were this soft and warm. Swaddled in them, Coo felt like she'd discovered another kind of summer.

"They're yours to keep," said Tully. "I knit far more than I know what to do with, anyway, especially now that I'm retired."

Coo crouched beside Tully, who watched her carefully.

"Okay, you?" Coo asked Burr. How strange it was to whisper into a dark box.

Burr's faint coos came from the shadows. "Okay, me. Be careful, you. Go back to the roof, you." He took a deep, ragged breath. "Quick!"

"Do you spend a lot of time with pigeons?" asked Tully, staring down at her.

Coo glanced at her warily.

"Coo's an unusual name," Tully continued. "Is it short for something?" Tully paused. "How about you tell me while we take a walk together to someplace safe?"

"Heal, you?" Coo whispered to Burr, ignoring the human babbling beside her. "Heal and return, you? Promise?"

"Only safe with flock, you." Burr's voice sounded faint. "Roof now, you! Go!"

Tears started to burn around Coo's eyelids. She took a few steps back, then a few more. Leaving Burr hurt more than the worst stubbed toe. More than ten stomachache mornings.

"Wait, don't go!" called Tully. "Coo!"

Coo turned and scampered to the fence. She crawled through the hole and hid behind the bushes. For the first time she took a good look at the side of her building. Some crumbling concrete steps, tangled with vines, led up to a hole in the wall bigger than the windows. It was half-covered in boards, too. A door of some kind. Mysterious.

"At least take these." Tully tossed another brown paper sack over the fence. "They were for my dessert, but I don't need them. I'm coming back as soon as possible with some help. Just hold on, little one!"

Coo peered through the bushes. Tully paced back and forth for what felt like a very long time, her face tight and frowning. Eventually she trudged out of sight.

Coo imagined Burr in the dark box, disappearing up the alley, around the corner, and then—she couldn't picture anything past that point. Her imagination's blankness grew and grew until it blotted out everything else. This was real, not like playing pretend games. Her heart pounded. She hunkered low against the scratchy ground and shut her eyes. At least she felt warm. Never in her life had she felt so warm when it was this cold outside. She pulled the soft red hat down over her ears and rubbed the scarf against her cheek.

"Come back, Burr will," said New Tiktik, flying over the fence and plopping down in front of Coo. "Like Hoop."

New Tiktik was trying to make her feel better. Coo forced herself to open her eyes.

"Come on, you," New Tiktik continued. "Back up, you. Getting colder now."

The sun had raced away across the sky, and the alley was deep in clammy shadow. A few flock members pecked at the last bits of seed scattered in the gravel, but most were already back on the roof. Coo remembered Burr's terror about her being down on the ground. It seemed more urgent than his fear about his broken wing. A shiver ran down Coo's spine.

What if there were bigger cats? Cats that ate humans? Coo jumped to her feet.

Somewhere up the alley, something growled. It sounded like the shiny things that zoomed over the gray ribbon on one side of the factory, but louder.

Cars. Unlike the trains that slinked slowly across the tracks nearby, cars weren't predictable. They scuttled fast all over the wide gray paths that ran between the buildings. Sometimes they hit pigeons. They didn't even eat them, just smashed them and kept going. Her flock was deeply wary of them.

Coo forgot all about giant cats. What if a car came around the bend right now? Maybe that's what Burr was warning about. It could smash *her*.

Getting back up to the roof seemed impossible—she hadn't thought that part through—but Coo gripped Tully's brown paper bag in her teeth and rushed back to the ladder anyway. The metal was colder now. It rubbed her palms raw as she struggled to haul herself up, step by freezing step. She reached the first landing, where the stairs began, and sighed with relief.

"Back, you?" Roohoo looked down at her from the next landing. "Not staying with humans, you? Too bad."

Coo started to cry. But there was nothing less

pigeon-like than tears. She didn't dare let Roohoo see them. He was the sort of pigeon who noticed differences like that. She stopped and closed her eyes.

Suddenly fear gripped her, a new kind of fear. The world was so much bigger than the roof. She couldn't fly. What if she fell?

When she opened her eyes again, twilight had come. Below her, something rustled in the bushes.

"Flock?" she called, hoping someone would swoop down to join her on her climb back up to the roof. "New Tiktik? Hoop?"

Most pigeons hated leaving the dovecote at night, but she called again. Coo was different, after all. She was important. Wouldn't someone come to check on her?

"Hem? Ka?"

No one responded.

"Can't hear me, them," Coo said out loud, her voice shaky. "Must be it."

Loneliness enveloping her like the evening shadows, Coo steeled herself and started climbing again. At last she reached the safety of the roof and scrambled through the darkness into the sleepy warmth of the dovecote.

Chapter Four
Officers

Coo was so distraught over Burr, and numbly bewildered by her terrifying trip to the ground and back, that she forgot all about looking inside Tully's brown paper sack until late that evening. The sun had long since set, and the sky was a chilly purple. In the rail yard the big evening lamps were lit, bathing the tracks in yellow.

Coo discovered three more exquisite donuts inside the sack. One was creamy white, like clean feathers, and dotted with perfect orange sprinkles; one was palest pink, like a good sunrise; and the third was a rich blackish brown.

It could have been dirt, like the dirt that collected in the roof corners, but Coo knew otherwise. Her heart soared. *Chocolate!* Chocolate was rare. Pigeons didn't like it. They didn't even like carrying it in their beaks from the dumpster, and Roohoo made fun of her for asking for it. She'd have Tully's chocolate donut all to herself, she decided.

Rare donut in hand, she wiggled out of the dovecote to sit on the roof ledge. She huddled under some newspaper and slowly licked the frosted top, looking out at the world beyond. She stared down at the wide gray ribbon and shuddered as a car zoomed over it. How much bigger and stranger and more terrifying the world was now than it had been this morning. Her head hurt just thinking about it. Cats. Humans. Tiny skies.

How could Tully keep Burr safe in such a world?

Hoop had tried to soothe her by describing

what she could of Tully, but Coo dwelled on Little Beak, one of the pigeons Tully had taken years ago who had never returned. She thought about the box Burr had disappeared into and the bend in the alley where Tully had vanished. She swallowed a chunk of donut.

Where was he right now? Was he safe and warm? It was very cold outside. Was he in pain? She imagined him lying somewhere alone and hurting, abandoned by Tully, and lost her appetite.

She looked toward the dovecote. The pigeons seemed to have forgotten about Burr. That was their way. The flock always mattered more than any one pigeon. Always had and always would.

Coo tucked the half-finished donut back into the bag with the ones she planned to share with the flock for breakfast. She was about to shimmy inside the dovecote when she turned back to look at the roof. It was exactly the same, but also somehow different. The moon had risen, full and merry, casting cool light over everything familiar:

red chair, pile of pebbles, tall weeds.

Her eye fell on the solid, hulking tower that had always lurked in the center of the roof. One side had a reddish-orange rectangle set into it, and when she was bored Coo often shoved bits of twigs and rocks through the mysterious small gaps that ran around it. When the roof's wildflowers bloomed, she liked to pick them and stick them into the gaps, too. The white and yellow blossoms looked very pretty against the rust color. Now she recognized the rectangle. It was like the plywood-covered hole in the side of the factory, above the crumbling steps.

A door. Where did it go?

Coo tiptoed toward it, her bare toes curling against the cold. She reached for the metal ball that stuck out from a stem on one side of it, and tugged. Over the years she had pushed and tugged on it many times without anything happening. This time was no different. It did not budge.

Suddenly she felt very tired. Shivering, she

hurried back to the dovecote and crawled into her nest. She stared out the dovecote's opening at the soft, blurry ridges of the skyline twinkling far in the distance. The buildings' starry little lights glowed brighter than the real stars scattered in the sky. She gazed at them for a long time.

"Different now," Coo whispered to no one in particular. "Everything different."

She watched tiny orbs of light glide high up in the sky on the flight paths she knew by heart. Strange birds those were. Tonight she couldn't stop looking at them and wondering about things the pigeons couldn't quite explain. Human things.

Packed tight in the shelves of the dovecote all around her, the flock slumbered. Coo had never in her life felt so alone. She had never felt so human.

Many hours passed before she fell asleep.

The next morning Coo waited a long time in the alley. The sun came up over the sides of the building. New Tiktik and Hoop, who had accompanied her down to the ground with Old Tiktik and Roohoo, grew restless and fluttered back up to the dovecote.

Tully was very late today. Coo thought about trying to walk up the alley herself. Maybe Tully was just beyond the bend where the alley disappeared behind the buildings. Maybe Burr was there, too. Maybe there were donuts.

Coo stood up from the sunny patch of gravel where she'd been squatting. She took a few steps forward. Then a few more. She was nearly at the corner when she heard Tully's voice.

The healer was not alone. Coo heard slamming sounds and other voices, deep ones. Human feet came crunching up the gravel. Heavy feet, not like Tully's at all. Coo scrambled back to the fence. The hairs stood up along the back of her neck. She needed to hide.

The pigeons sensed it, too.

"More humans," said Old Tiktik, from her perch on the fence. "Odd, this."

"Whole human flock," said Roohoo when he returned from scouting around the bend. "Human flocks, bad!"

Coo scampered back as far as she could into the bushes. Tully's red hat caught on a thorny branch. She quickly took it off and stuck it down the front of her plastic romper. Luckily there was an evergreen that never lost its dark green needles, and she was soon well hidden behind its scratchy bulk. Peering between branches, she still had a decent view of the alley.

Coo had thought Tully was large, but the two other humans coming down the alley with her were *huge*. They towered over Tully. They wore dark blue pants and shirts with many metallic glinting bits. Many more heavy-looking metal things dangled around their waists. One held a crackling metal box in its hand.

"You really shouldn't be back here in the first place, ma'am," one of the humans said.

"Feeding pigeons is not illegal, Officer," said Tully.

"It's not, but this property belongs to the city. No trespassing."

"Okay, now I know. But the girl!" Tully raised her hands in the air, palms up. "I'm afraid she's been abandoned here. Or she has a family that is not caring for her properly. She's filthy and neglected!"

"Ms. Tully, you said she was about what, eleven? Height, weight, race?"

"Short, Officer. Painfully thin. White. Brownish, matted hair. Very suntanned. Boyish, but I'm almost sure she's a girl. As I said, she doesn't seem to speak English. She just gobbled up the food I gave her like a stray dog."

"She hangs out in the alley here? You sure she's only eleven?"

"She might even be younger. Whoever is caring for her is doing a terrible job. I would take her in myself."

"Getting ahead of yourself there, sweetie."

"Fine. Whatever." Tully frowned. "Just please look for her! It's much too cold for her to be out here in nothing but a plastic bag and the hat and scarf I gave her."

One officer was holding a small rectangle and scribbling on it with a stick. "We'll poke around," he said.

"She ran into the bushes when she got scared," said Tully, pointing directly to the place where Coo was hiding. "Over there."

The two strangers clomped and crunched across the gravel toward Coo. The few lingering pigeons heaved up and headed in a wave toward the roof. But Coo couldn't go with them. She had to stay put, still as no breeze, and hope these big scowling humans didn't see her.

She almost made it. But just as the officers reached the fence, the crackling metal box one held in his hand suddenly began to speak. It had a voice. Like a human! It took all Coo had inside her not to scream. But she did jump. The bush shook.

"Aha!" cried Tully. "She's there. Come out, Coo! It's safe. These policemen are here to help you."

At the very same moment, a streak of gray fuzz shot out from another bush and right through the hole in the fence. Yowling, it zipped past the policemen and Tully and disappeared up the alley.

It was the cat that had nearly eaten Burr, and for the first time, Coo was grateful for it.

"Are you sure you saw a kid, ma'am? Not a cat or a raccoon or something?"

The two officers laughed.

Tully did not laugh. She looked anxious. "Of course I know a child from a wild animal," she said.

"Well, next time call us as soon as you see her. Or rabid raccoons or anything. Here's my card." One of the officers handed Tully a small flat piece of paper. "Or bring her to the precinct, if she'll come with you. Good luck with that, though. It sounds like she's a truant."

"A truant?"

"Skipping school. There have been some car break-ins around here, and someone reported seeing a kid loitering near one of 'em. White, thin. Maybe it's the kid you saw."

"Listen, Officer," said Tully. "She is a child. All by herself. This is serious. You aren't going to search for her?"

The officers began to trudge back up the alley. Tully trailed behind. They continued to babble. None of it made sense, though Coo could muddle through some of the tones—joking and impatient from the two strangers, anxious and sad from Tully.

"We'll check tomorrow, okay? If you see her again, we can do a full search of the building," said one of the officers. "So far there haven't been any other reports. And no missing kids or teens fitting your description. But keep in touch with us, okay? We'll fill out a report in the cruiser."

They vanished around the bend and their voices faded.

Coo let go of the branch she'd been clutching and realized she'd gripped it so hard she'd drawn blood. She licked her wound, watching the alley.

Coo did not dare go down to the ground again. Not later that day, when Tully returned alone, scattering seed and calling Coo's name over and over. Not the next day, when more officers arrived and stomped and peered and shouted all over the alley and even inside the building below her, hitting the fence with black sticks and barking into their crackling boxes. Nor did she go down in the days that followed, each colder than the last, when Tully appeared looking sadder and sadder, and called Coo's name in a quieter and quieter voice.

Coo mostly stayed cooped up in the dovecote. It felt safest. Chilled rain came, and she burrowed more deeply into her nest, trying hard not to think about Burr, or her curiosity about Tully.

She held out a crumb of hope for Burr. Hoop, the one who had been to the secret and mysterious place where the healer took sick birds, assured Coo again and again that Tully was a good human, and the gruff humans with their sticks and boxes had never appeared during Hoop's time with her.

"Safe with human, me," said Hoop. "Dry. Warm. Foot, healed. Gentle, human."

"Hungry there, you?"

"Never. Kind, the human."

"Maybe," snorted Roohoo. "Trust a human, us? Really? Kick, humans do. Always kick."

"Hush, Roohoo," said Old Tiktik. "Kind, some humans. Coo, Tully, both very kind."

It took a long time to heal, Hoop said. Many days and nights. Burr would be back, someday. Coo just had to wait.

Chapter Five
Hunger

"Gone," the pigeons said one cold morning a few days after Burr disappeared with Tully. The roof sparkled with new frost. They'd returned to the roof with no bagels or donuts or even bread rolls in their beaks. "Dumpster gone."

Resorting to pecking at the spills around the small bins on the sidewalks, they'd only found scraps. Nothing worth hauling back for Coo.

"Hungry, me," said Pook, a particularly

impatient yearling. "Bagels? Please?"

This wasn't the first time a dumpster had disappeared. Coo's stomach rumbled loudly just thinking about it. Long ago, there had been a closer dumpster, one that yielded much more than bagels and donuts: it had bananas, bread, cupcakes, cheese, all in clear sacks that two pigeons working together could haul the short block back to the roof.

Memories of those foods lived in Coo's memory like a distant summer.

Coo had never seen any kind of dumpster in person, and the pigeons weren't particularly clear in describing how they looked except that they were the same color as the roof, so she spent hours and hours imagining them: big shining grayish clouds on the ground that spit out delicious food.

Until they didn't. One day the pigeons had gone to that dumpster, the one with such miraculous variety, and discovered it had vanished. Flown away. Dissolved.

Hunger

The days that followed had turned into weeks of gnawing, headache-making, frightening hunger, a long, terrible time spent living on nothing more than a few muffin crumbs from a sidewalk trash bin or a beakful of raw dough from an unreliable dumpster far away, before the pigeons found the new one. The bagel-and-donut one.

Now that dumpster had vanished, too. Coo's heart quickened. She tucked Tully's red hat snugly over her ears, then retied the brown scarf. Whenever she was worried, she rubbed the scarf's soft ends against her cheek, and it helped her calm down.

"Back tomorrow?" she asked hopefully. "One gone day, not so bad?"

"Dumpsters? No," said Roohoo. "Gone now, gone always."

"Hush," said Hoop. "Maybe."

But Roohoo was right. The pigeons returned over and over, at all hours, for days, but the bagel-and-donut dumpster had disappeared for good.

~ ~ ~

"Eat, you." Ka dropped a mushy, blackish-yellow object at Coo's feet. A banana. She hadn't seen one in so long it was hard to remember what they tasted like.

This one was brown and purple inside and nearly beginning to rot. Coo inhaled it. It was the first big meal she'd had in more than a week.

"Grateful, me," she said between bites. "Thank you, Ka."

"Searching hard for you, us," he said. "Hungry, too, me. Hungry, all."

"Know it, me." Coo's cheeks burned. She stopped chewing and hastily pushed the last bits of banana toward Ka. "Grateful, me. Very grateful."

It wasn't like the flock to expend so much energy on just one member. Coo suddenly felt huge and helpless, like a ridiculously overgrown squab refusing to leave the nest. When Burr was around, she'd never felt this way, not once. He always reminded the rest of them how much she mattered and made her feel special. But Burr was gone. Maybe forever. And hardly anyone else seemed to notice or care.

Even New Tiktik was acting a little distant and tired.

"Hard work looking for food," she said when she brought Coo a soggy, flattened muffin one rainy morning a few days later. "Can't eat seed, you? Really?"

Coo had long ago discovered that the seed Tully scattered most days did nothing but give her tummy aches. The pigeons still tried bringing her some from time to time, and she felt bad turning it down, especially when they had to look so hard for anything else.

Half-gnawed bagels, torn and dried pizza slices, a few banana chunks. The flock flew farther and farther every day to find food for themselves, and most of the time it was too far to bring anything back for Coo. One evening New Tiktik dared to steal a craggy brown apple core from a squirrel in the rail yard, and Coo ate it gratefully, even though it tasted vile.

She had stopped playing Find Food. No pigeon besides Burr was ever very encouraging about it, but now the others avoided her when she started. It was sad playing alone. Besides that, pretending about food was no fun when you wanted the real kind and couldn't have it. Looking at rocks that were supposed to be donuts made Coo's hunger pains worse.

"Miss Burr, me," she said wistfully.

"Find him, you," said New Tiktik. "Down on the ground. Get food, too."

"What? Cats there. Cars there. Scary! No."

"Not scary," said New Tiktik. "Go on, you. Ask human, you. About food and Burr."

"Can't ask human, me. Remember? Don't speak human."

It confused New Tiktik as much as it did Coo. If Coo was really a human, like Roohoo said, why couldn't she understand Tully? Pigeons never had trouble understanding other pigeons, even from different flocks.

Coo puzzled over this again, rubbing her head, but it was hard to think when she was so hungry.

"Give you food anyway, Tully." New Tiktik and the other pigeons knew the healer's human name now. "Show you Burr, too, her. Both humans, you. Go down."

"Don't want to, me."

Coo thought of the strangers Tully had brought into the alley and shuddered.

"Starve on roof, you." Ka landed next to her. "All struggling, us."

"Get her own food, Coo," Roohoo said, hopping down next to Ka. "Human, she is! Remember?"

Coo stared at her hands. The air was frigid. Her fingers were thin and red.

Ka wasn't mean like Roohoo, but he was stern.

"Not a squab, you," Ka said quietly. "Time to get food like a big pigeon, you."

The next morning Coo stared over the edge of the roof, looking for Tully. The healer came less and less frequently these days. Coo was growing so weak, it hurt to think about climbing down the fire escape. Her stomach was as dry and empty as a broken eggshell.

At last she heard Tully coming down the alley. She peeked over the side and watched her scatter the birdseed. Hungry, every last flock member zoomed down to eat. Coo was alone on the roof.

She leaned over the fire escape, hesitating. Without New Tiktik to encourage her, or Ka to nudge her, the trip down was daunting. Worse, she felt dizzy. She steadied herself and closed her eyes.

Suddenly she heard Tully's voice.

"Coo! Is that you on the roof? I see your hat!"

Coo startled. All at once her head felt as light as a plastic bag twirling in the wind. She sunk down against the low wall that ran around the roof and closed her eyes. Tully's voice sounded very far away. She thought about Burr and other sick pigeons she'd known. How frightening it was to feel ill! She tried to call for her flock, but panic stole her voice.

She lay curled in a ball for a long time. Eventually Tully stopped calling for her. The flock returned from feasting in the alley. Most of them ignored her, but New Tiktik and Hoop brought her some sweet crumbs they'd found a few blocks away. It was enough to revive her so she could stagger back to the dovecote. None of the other pigeons talked to her.

With Burr gone, she had learned things about the flock and her place in it that she'd never known—or wanted to know—before. Some of it was going to be hard to forget.

Chapter Six
Snow

The next morning the air felt unusually thick and still. There was something ominous about it. Even Coo could feel it where she huddled deep in her nest. But it was too soon for snow, so she didn't worry.

"Storm," said New Tiktik, zooming in and out of the doorway. The pigeons always knew the weather before Coo did. Even young ones like New Tiktik. "Big snow! Soon."

Snow. The worst word. Heart pounding, Coo stumbled out onto the roof. The sky was heavy and gray. The clouds were so dense and low that the faraway skyline and its lights had disappeared. The air was frigid. Coo shivered, and not just from the cold. She was scared. Really scared.

"Snow?" Coo asked Hoop anxiously. "Too early. Leaves on trees, now."

Snow rarely came before all the leaves were gone from the trees Coo could see from the roof, and quite a few brown, red, and yellow ones still hung on the branches.

"Snow," Hoop replied. "Much snow."

Scarier than hawks, scarier than metal-jangling human strangers, scarier than anything, was snow.

Coo's earliest storms were icy whirlwinds, pigeons blanketing her three birds deep in the dovecote to keep her from freezing to death. As she grew, she learned to burrow into her nest, pile on insulating newspapers, and wait it out in chilled fear.

Just the year before she had survived a bad blizzard: two nights and three days trapped inside the dovecote with only half a soggy sesame bagel and barely enough old clumps of newspaper packed around her to save her from turning into an icicle.

Even after that horrible storm stopped howling, it took weeks for the snow to melt off the roof and months for Coo's bones to really warm up. And that was back when she had regular food. And Burr, who always looked out for her.

Who would look out for her now?

She stared across the roof toward the alley.

Tully.

Ever since she'd become dizzy trying to climb onto the fire escape, she'd been too weak and scared to try to return to the alley. But now there was a storm coming.

Could Tully give her some food and more things like the hat and scarf to keep warm? Maybe Tully even knew how to stop the snow before it arrived. Could humans do that?

"Tully!" Coo hobbled across the roof and called down into the alley. "Help me, you! Tully!"

No one replied. The alley was deserted.

Coo shivered, and her stomach rumbled. If Tully came, would she even have the strength to climb down the fire escape?

A few snowflakes whirled from the sky. Coo gave one last look at the alley and stumbled back into the dovecote.

Coo awoke blinking and shivering. Something cold and sharp was prickling her cheeks. Her hair was damp and heavy. So was the rest of her body.

Snow! Lots of it. Just like the pigeons had said. Coo tottered to her feet. Clumps of snow tumbled from her body. She was numb with cold every-where except for her head and neck, which were covered by Tully's hat and scarf.

While she'd slept, the wind had lashed great

drifts across the roof and into the doorway. The dovecote shook. Pigeons muttered around her.

No matter what happened, the flock would survive. Snow was one of those things that pigeons—healthy ones—handled better than humans.

The wind gusted another spray of ice pellets onto Coo's cheeks. Suddenly she wondered about Burr. If he was still alive, was he warm and dry? Was Tully keeping him safe?

"Storm. Not good," Coo whispered. "Bad, bad, bad."

At the sound of her voice, pigeons hopped down from their perches and huddled around her.

"Poor you," said Hoop. "No feathers." She extended her brownish dappled wing over Coo's shivering shoulder.

"Scared, me," Coo murmured.

The snow was colder and icier than it had ever been before. How was that possible? She closed her eyes. Time was different, too—it was slower.

She thought of the sandwich Tully had given

her. She thought of Tully's face and her soft hands, and her voice. Coo pulled the red hat so far down over her face it almost reached her mouth.

The wind screamed past the dovecote, shrill as a cat, and Coo jumped.

She started to cry, then made herself stop. Tears froze and hurt her skin.

"Stay warm, you." New Tiktik landed on Coo's head and nuzzled her ears. "Okay, you. Strong, you."

Kind words helped.

Coo took a shuddering breath. Storms always ended. Snow always melted. It was just a matter of getting through it.

Hours passed. Coo got very sleepy. She fought to stay awake. She knew sleep was bad. Weak, sick pigeons who fell asleep in storms never woke up. She blinked and pinched herself.

Suddenly there was a great *bang* as if a part of the roof had collapsed. The pigeons lifted up in the air, jumbling together in the dovecote, and settled back on their perches. Coo's hands, despite their numbness, began to tremble. She had never in all her years heard such a noise on the roof.

"Coo!" a faint human voice shouted. "Where are you? Goodness, what is a dovecote doing on this old roof? Coo? Are you in that thing?"

Coo pushed through the snow and wind until her head poked through the doorway. Night had fallen. The whole world shrieked with swirling snow. She squinted and blinked as a plump black shape, a big garbage bag with legs, appeared in the whirlwind. A bright beam of light zigzagged around it. It flashed directly into Coo's eyes, blinding her, and then vanished.

"Coo!" the garbage bag screamed.

Tully!

"I knew I'd seen you on this roof! Those police officers wouldn't come check," Tully said as she stumbled to the dovecote. "You live here? All alone? My God!"

Tully pulled Coo into a warm hug and stuck her head through the door. "Hello? Is anyone in there?"

The flock hooted softly.

"Oh, you poor baby. You would have died! Come with me. Hurry."

They staggered over the rooftop snowdrifts toward the tower with the forever-shut door.

Now the tower had a big black hole in one side, and the door was a flap of metal swinging in the snowy wind.

"Going, you?" Tiny New Tiktik, just a ball of gray struggling to stay aloft in the howling wind, had followed Coo out into the storm. "Where, Coo?"

"Back to the dovecote, you!" Coo cried. "Too windy!"

New Tiktik bobbed for a moment, then turned and zoomed into the wall of snow. She would make it to the dovecote just fine, Coo knew. Healthy young pigeons always did.

But humans? What happened when they left the dovecote?

Coo took a deep breath. She was alone with Tully now. Whatever happened next was beyond anything she'd imagined.

Tully pushed Coo through the doorway and slammed the slab of metal behind them. They plunged into a silent pitch-blackness. Never had Coo been in such darkness.

Just as suddenly there was light. A shocking yellow glow emanated from a black bar Tully gripped in her left mitten. The wild zigzagging light had been coming from Tully's hand. Sunlight on a stick!

"Holy moly!" said Tully. "You're wearing nothing but plastic bags and my old hat and scarf. Take my coat. Quickly!"

Tully pulled off the black thing she wore and wrapped it around Coo. It was heavy, and so long it dragged on the floor, but it was also warm and soft. Coo's deep shivering slowed.

"Maybe I should call an ambulance. Can you walk? Try."

Coo followed as Tully began clunking her way

down a dark and musty iron staircase. Coo's snowy plastic-bag shoes slipped and slid, and Tully gripped her hand tight.

Inside the building! Under the roof! Despite the hunger and cold, Coo craned her neck to look around. It was spooky. Tully's flashlight illuminated a dusty, paint-peeling, abandoned world, a place full of shadows. Coo did not like the inside of the building, she decided.

Tully led her all the way down the stairs and through the now-open doorway into the snowy corridor between the factory and the fence. Coo was relieved to be outside again, even in the howling wind and snow. Tully helped Coo sit on the snowy step while she stomped around looking for the fence rip. When she found it, she pushed Coo through and then wiggled out after her.

"It's just as well you're wearing my coat; I barely fit!" Tully huffed, pulling her legs through and standing up again. "Now, I think

I can carry you, at least until we reach the plowed street."

Coo was alarmed, but too weak to protest, when Tully swooped her off her feet and began trudging up the alley. For the first time, Coo went beyond the bend. The alley led to a loosely chained gate made from the same material as the fence. Still holding Coo, Tully wiggled through the gap, then put Coo down.

A rumble like the loudest train Coo had ever heard rolled past them, and snow was flung in all directions. "Snowplow!" Tully shouted. "Don't be scared! Can you walk now?"

Coo clung to Tully's sweater sleeve as they stumbled over the drifts and onto the plowed street. Maybe Tully was taking her to the same place she took sick birds, like Hoop said she would. Maybe she healed humans, too.

"I told the police I'd bring you straight to the precinct if I found you, but I just can't do it. Not tonight." Tully shook her head. "I don't know what they'll do with you or where they'll send you. Even though it sure would be satisfying to see the look on their faces when they have to admit I wasn't seeing things."

Coo focused entirely on walking, not bothering to try to decipher what Tully was saying. The street was clear of snow, but very slippery with slush and ice. Coo looked up. The buildings had dropped away, and they were passing a wide, flat field of nothing but snow.

"Even Food Bazaar closed for this blizzard," Tully said when she saw Coo looking at it. "I've never seen their parking lot so empty."

Tully coaxed her along, babbling brightly.

"We're almost there now, Coo. We just crossed the big road, and soon we'll be on my block. Just another few steps. Then we'll go inside and get you warmed up." Tully's voice was soothing. "I'll call the police in the morning, when I've figured out exactly what to say. Back when Ben had his accident, they—well, we won't get into that. It's just hard for me to trust them. Especially during a blizzard like this."

They reached a quiet street of scrunched-together buildings. Cars piled up with snow sat still and dark along the edges of the road like frosted buns. The snow was everywhere, swirling in the yellow lights that sat on tall poles. Coo looked around. She was almost delirious with hunger and cold, but still curious.

Food, Coo thought. Maybe there would be food. It was the only way to keep herself upright.

"This is my building," Tully said, lifting Coo up a snow-covered slope of steps and through a heavy brown door.

The howling of the wind quieted. They walked along a short hallway to a pale blue door with a faded flower-print mat in front of it.

"Welcome to my apartment, Coo."

Coo stepped inside. Her thoughts of food vanished. She gasped.

Chapter Seven
Tully's Home

"Burr!" Coo rushed to the cube of thin twigs that sat on a table in the corner. "Healed, you?" She pressed her face against the cage and inhaled Burr's familiar scent. "Trapped, you!"

"Not trapped, me," said Burr. "Cage opens. Can't fly, me." He lifted his limp left wing, and with horror Coo saw it hung askew from the side of his body. A tiny pink and green length of knitting, like a miniature scarf, wound around it up to

Burr's neck and kept the wing from brushing the ground. Coo had never seen such a thing.

Pigeons who couldn't fly died fast.

"No," Coo whispered. "Not still broken, you. No."

"Yes, broken. Always broken now. Don't worry, you. Safe here, me. Helps me, Tully's string," he said, and pecked the little scarf.

"But can't fly, you!" Coo was on the verge of tears. "Hawks! Cats!"

"No hawks here. No cats."

"Are you—are you two communicating?" Tully's eyes were large as donuts. "You *were* living alone with those pigeons in that old pigeon coop."

Coo stared at her, cautious. She had never seen a face that looked so shocked. What if the strangers covered in metal were on their way? She sized up Burr's cage, and Tully's doorway. But then her stomach rumbled. Her knees felt flimsier than newspaper. And it was snowing. There was no place to run. She knew she couldn't make it to the alley, much less climb the fire escape.

At least she and Burr were together. And he was alive.

"I've heard stories about kids raised by animals," Tully continued, blinking rapidly. "Mostly bears, or maybe tigers? I remember in school learning about the legend of the twin boys raised by wolves in ancient Italy. One of them ended up founding the city of Rome. But they were myths. And none were about pigeons. Pigeons! It's just not possible."

Tully looked alarmed. She rubbed her temples. "But who left you with them? Where are your parents? Oh, the neglect!"

"So loud, her," Coo whispered to Burr.

"Loud, humans are," Burr replied. "Loud, too, you."

Coo rattled the bars of Burr's cage.

"Free!" she shouted at Tully in pigeon. "Free him, you!"

"Here I am muttering to myself about all this

when you want to see your friend. I'm sorry, Coo. Here you go." Tully lumbered to her feet. She fiddled with some wires on Burr's cage and a door opened among the bars.

"Go on," she said to Coo. "He's out of danger now. I knit him a little sling, which seems to help his wing stay comfortable."

Coo shimmied out of Tully's big coat and reached into the wire box. At once she and Burr were together again. He nestled against her chilly arms, his feathers soft and warm against her cold skin.

"Happy," said Coo, trembling. "I'm so happy."

"Me too," said Burr.

"You really are speaking to him. Oh, what on earth am I going to do with you? I can't hand you over to strangers now. What will your life be like if it's discovered how you were surviving?" Tully put her head in her hands. "I wish my dear Ben was here to help."

Tully stood up and began opening and shutting doors and disappearing into other rooms. Coo

looked up from the sheer
joy of cuddling Burr to study
her. What was she doing?

"At the very least I can help you
clean up and get into some soft,
normal clothes," Tully said when
she returned holding a pile of
cloth. "Not those disgusting
plastic bags! Come, let's go to the bathroom."

When Tully reached for her, motioning for her
to hand Burr over, Coo recoiled.

"No, you!" Coo shouted in pigeon. She
tucked Burr against her chest and dashed
behind a chair.

"Hide, why? Safe here, you," said Burr. "Kind,
she is."

Coo was too exhausted and confused to argue
with him.

"I see I'm going to have to win your trust." Tully
sighed. "You must be hungry."

A few minutes later, Tully crouched down in

front of the chair holding a small apple.

"Apple? Do you know apples?" Tully mimed taking a big bite.

A whole apple. Round as a doorknob and green as a new leaf. Coo looked at it in wonder. She had only ever had them half-bitten, smashed, or chewed down to the core.

"You eat it," Tully said, handing it to her. "We'll do a bath and new clothes tomorrow. I'll go back to the kitchen to figure out more food for you now."

That night, after eating the perfect green apple, six strawberries, and a pile of flaky, sticky squares Tully called peanut butter crackers, and drinking water that tasted cleaner than fresh rain, Coo felt safe enough to crawl out from behind the chair. Tully led her to a small, dark room and helped her curl up on a narrow plank that sat against one wall. Burr napped beside her with his head tucked under his crooked wing.

Tully slumbered in the main room, on the wide,

soft, pink-and-white chair she said was called a loveseat.

The blizzard and the wild trek through the snow had tired her to the bone, but Coo lay wide-awake for a long time. Her stomach was full for the first time in ages, but the spongy plank under her was peculiar. She worried she would sink through it, right to the floor. The warm things Tully called blankets smelled good, but some shredded newspaper and plastic bags would have made her more comfortable. By themselves the blankets were so flat and clean it made her nervous.

Coo could see snow swirling and wind-battered trees through a window covered in a solid puddle of clear ice—the kind of window Roohoo complained about. It was very cold to the touch. Yet it didn't crack, no matter how hard she tapped it.

"Odd, here," Coo murmured. She lifted Burr's wing, careful not to undo his sling, to peer into his sleepy face.

"Safe, you," cooed Burr. "Happy, me. Sleep now, you."

Coo smiled at him. Burr was very different from her, but he was still the most important person in the world. She nestled down into the blankets next to him, forgetting how distant she was now from the flock.

The next morning Coo blinked awake. It was winter, but she wasn't cold. She was inside, but it was bright, not dim. It wasn't a dovecote. It was a room in the place where Tully lived, the place where sick pigeons went to heal. She shut her eyes and the previous day spun around her like the heavy snow.

"Here, me!" Burr cooed.

He was right beside her, cocking his head back and forth.

"Sleep long, you," he said. "Wait, me."

"Up now, me." Swiftly Coo scooped him into her arms for a cuddle. Out of all the shocking events since the blizzard began, finding Burr alive was the most stunning. She remembered how Old Tiktik and some of the others had thought she shouldn't even try to bring him to Tully. What if she had listened to them? She shuddered deep inside.

"Find Tully, you," said Burr. "Food here! Every morning."

Coo stood up and plopped Burr on her shoulder. Then she crept to the open doorway. Food, indeed. It smelled a bit like donuts. Rich and sweet.

Tully hovered over a squat green thing in the corner of the big room.

"Come eat," said Tully. "The stove's doing a good job warming up the place today."

Coo sat down on a chair at the round flat circle that Tully gestured to. The table, Tully called it. It was covered in a flowery cloth. She was surprised that things besides humans wore clothing. The night before she'd been too overwhelmed to really look at Tully's home. Now she peered around curiously.

There was the small table where Coo sat. There were two more big clear windows filled with snow. In front of one, on a ledge, was a round little brown pot with a green plant growing in it. Near the windows were a big blue chair all piled up with things like Coo's hat and scarf, and a smaller green chair that was empty. Coo was startled to find that chairs came in colors and materials other than the faded red plastic of the one she'd grown up with on the roof.

Above Burr's table and cage was a set of shelves—just like dovecote shelves—stacked with a dozen flat, bright slabs. Tiny black marks covered them, just like on newsprint. Interesting.

Coo hopped up from the chair by the food and scrambled over to the table beneath the shelves. She hopped up on that, reaching for the shelf and—

"No!" Tully barked sharp as a seagull.

Hands grabbed Coo under her armpits and dragged her back down.

"Dangerous!" Tully's mouth was a deep frown. "Climbing," she said slowly. "Fall. Hurt. Ouch. Understand?"

Coo stared back. Tully's words were beginning to make some kind of sense. Somehow she knew Tully meant she wasn't supposed to stand on the table. But it wasn't just her words. It was also the way her eyebrows shifted, and her mouth moved, and even how her shoulders tensed and relaxed. Pigeons communicated some things in the way they puffed their feathers or bent their heads, but it was nowhere near as complex as what humans did with their faces and bodies.

"Sit down at the table again," Tully said, pointing. "Before the pancakes get cold."

Pancakes. Tully nudged a spiky metal rod in Coo's direction, but Coo brushed it aside to quickly pick up the whole buttery, sticky stack of flat bread in both hands and take a giant bite. Sweetness. And a shock. The pancakes were hot! Like the rooftop on a summer day.

"I see you need to learn how to use forks and spoons." The corners of Tully's mouth twitched. She turned and flipped another pancake on the stove. "Most people don't eat pancakes with their hands."

"Food, good," Coo said in pigeon, her mouth so full of warm pancake it was hard to speak. Burr hopped down from her shoulder to peck up the soft crumbs falling all around her plate. Then he hobbled over to the edge of the table so Tully, smiling, could pop more little pancake scraps into his beak.

"I wonder how long I can wait to call the police about you, Coo, without them considering it kidnapping," Tully said. She had finished cooking and sat down at the table to eat her own pancakes. Her face had become dense with lines and a deep frown. "Considering how long they took to do anything after Ben's accident, I don't imagine they'd look too carefully into it."

Coo inhaled the last bit of pancake on her plate.

"But first—bath time. You shouldn't have to spend another moment in your own filth. Or those plastic bags!"

Still not understanding nearly everything Tully said, Coo suspected nothing when Tully ushered her and Burr into a tiny white room near the front door.

"Here's the bathroom. You're going to take a shower. Water. Soap. Clean!"

Coo wasn't listening. She was staring in utter shock at a strange slab stuck like a strange window on the wall. It was the clearest puddle she'd ever seen, more vivid than the cleanest, freshest ice. In it she saw Tully, who was holding Burr, and then a face she knew—almost—from the puddles on the roof. But it wasn't greenish brown and vague with leaves and sticks and grit. She reached her hand up and touched her nose. The figure in the wall touched its nose.

"Me!" Coo pressed her hands against her reflection. "Me! Coo!"

On her head, brown hair, browner than autumn leaves. It was matted thick, like the tumbleweed tangles in the roof corners, and trailed down her back. Her skin was tan and pink and streaked with brown and gray patches. Her eyes were what startled her the most. They were just like Tully's. Spring-sky blue.

"Me!" she said out loud again.

"Yes, a mirror," said Tully. "We might as well get the washing up part over with. Come, stand in the tub." She helped Coo out of her dirty plastic bags and then lifted her into a little room-within-the-room she called the bathtub. Then she turned some silvery knobs in the walls.

What happened next was the warmest, most terrible rainstorm Coo had ever been through. Hot water poured through the ceiling while Coo covered her eyes, too frightened to scream. She waited for the booming thunder and flashing lightning that nearly always accompanied such downpours, but astonishingly, they didn't come.

Worse than the fear of thunder and lightning, though, was the bitter-tasting white goop Tully rubbed all over her head and skin. It smelled almost, but not quite, like fresh flowers. Soap, Tully called it. Coo howled and pushed it away.

"Hush!" said Tully. "At the rate you're going, I won't need to call the cops; the neighbors will do it for me."

Coo kept her eyes shut tight and wished for the rain to end.

"No soap is enough to save this hair," Tully sighed. She turned the shiny knob in the wall again and the rain stopped. Then she wrapped Coo in a big soft cloth and helped her over to the mirror. "Come over here and hold very still."

Tully got out a sharp piece of metal and started snipping at Coo's head. Coo watched in horror as clumps of her matted hair fell to the floor. At the same time, she felt suddenly lighter.

"And we're done. See? Look in the mirror."

Coo looked up. The face that stared back at

her had changed again. Now it was scrubbed red. Clean. No more dirt marks. Her eyes looked less blue, but she looked past them, up to her head. She touched it. Gone was the rough, weedy tangle she'd always known. In its place was a short, almost feathery wave of brownish-yellow hair, still slightly damp to the touch.

Tully helped Coo get into something new and clean that Tully called clothes: soft stretchy leaf-green tubes that sagged over her legs and a large white flap of softness that went over her head and arms.

"Leggings and a sweatshirt. They're awfully large on you because they're mine," said Tully. "We'll get you proper clothes at Goodwill soon."

Coo looked in the mirror again. A dizzy feeling came over her, like she got from spinning in circles, or from the too-hot sun with no water on a late summer day.

Tully, cleaning up the towels and hair and plastic sacks on the floor, wasn't paying her any attention.

Burr had hopped out in the kitchen to eat the last of the breakfast scraps.

"Everything different now," whispered Coo, staring at herself. "Everything."

Whirling snow. Snow in her mouth. Snow burning her skin. Naked. No hat, no scarf. No plastic bags, even. Snow in the darkness. Snow everywhere.

Coo ran and ran and ran across the roof, but the dovecote never got any closer. No pigeons flew to meet her.

"Help me!" she screamed. "Help!"

Warm arms and a soft voice pulled her out of the nightmare.

"Hush. You're safe here. Shh. Everything is okay."

A light switched on. Yellow, like warm sun. Tully sat beside her on the squishy plank. She stroked Coo's hair. Burr hobbled across Coo's shoulder and nestled into the crook of Tully's arm.

Slowly, Coo woke up.

"Stay here, me!" Coo said urgently, sleepily. She couldn't go back into the cold. "Please!"

"Only pigeons know what you're saying, Coo," murmured Tully. "But don't worry. I've made up my mind. I'm going to take care of you. Nothing and no one will stop me. You're safe here now."

Chapter Eight
Goodwill

There was so much to learn. Everything was new.

Tully taught Coo about light switches, refrigerators, faucets, and stoves. The more Tully babbled, the more Coo began to understand her words. Tully showed Coo how to make the bed—*bed* was an easy word; it was a human's nest—and talked about going to the thrift store to find a little cot to make Coo's own, so Tully could get her own bed back.

But Coo preferred to sleep in a more pigeon-ish way. After a few nights, Tully understood and let her make a pile of clean blankets and cozy old newspapers in a corner of the living room.

Coo learned to drink water from a glass without spilling, fix a peanut butter sandwich, brush her teeth with sweet-tasting soap, and turn the shower on and off, discovering in the process that it was not as much like a thunderstorm as she first thought. Tully taught her how to use the rest of the bathroom, too.

Tully's house was full of mysteries. There were orbs of sunlight in the ceiling that turned on and off with a switch. There was a freezer, where food lay in piles of icy snow behind a plastic door.

There was endless food, all of it fresh and clean and tasty. The words Tully had for it were as delicious as the food itself.

Lemon cheesecake.

Fruit cocktail.

Tapioca pudding.

Oyster crackers.

Toast with strawberry jam—how strange! Humans made their bread hard and stale on purpose, then added rotten-looking fruit slime. Yet it somehow tasted good.

Cheddar cheese on saltines.

Buttered noodles.

Potato chips.

Shrimp lo mein and vegetable fried rice from something called Jade Moon Kitchen, which a man delivered in fragrant cartons right to Tully's door.

Coo had never imagined food could be so different and miraculous.

On a cloudy afternoon soon after she arrived, Coo watched in awe as Tully used two sticks and a big ball of stringy fluff to make a small red scarf for Coo, one to match the big red hat Coo refused to take off.

"I love having someone to knit for," said Tully,

her hands flying. "Ever since the postal service forced me to retire, I've been up to my ears in knitting, trying to kill time while I figure out what to do with my life. I've made some things for my little neighbor Aggie, but I'm not sure she wants ten more hats and a dozen scarves."

Burr was sitting on Coo's shoulder, and she reached out to touch his sling. He had many different ones, and Tully changed them almost every day. Today's sling was blue and white and covered in tiny bumps Tully called popcorn stitches.

"Oh yes." Tully laughed. "I love knitting for Milton, too, but there's only so much you can knit for a pigeon, even one as willing to wear my outfits as Milton."

A few mornings later, Coo woke up and found Tully frowning.

"The blizzard was a wonderful excuse to avoid taking you anywhere, but I have a long to-do list now. Including getting you to a doctor, I think.

You're terribly thin." She sighed and shook her head.
"But first, some shopping. I can't knit all of your
clothes, and you need a winter coat. We're going to
Goodwill. Luckily it's right around the corner."

Tully pulled two matching pink objects with
flat bottoms off a shelf. "Temporary shoes," said
Tully. "I found these in the free pile in the laundry
room a few days ago. They look almost your size.
And here's the smallest pair of socks I own."

Clumsily, Coo rolled the socks over her rough,
wild feet. Tully ripped open the tops of the shoes—
they made a gnashing sound and Coo jumped—
and Coo pushed in one foot, and then the other. It
felt like stuffing them into a stale bagel.

"Sneakers," Tully said slowly. "See? Now you can
walk and not get cold or hurt. Less slippery, too."

Coo wiggled her toes. Her feet were strange and
tamed, and standing felt like floating.

It was odd to be outside again. Tully had bundled
her in several layers of too-big sweaters, and for

the first time ever she was walking around in winter without feeling cold. The air was fresh and familiar, and felt good to breathe.

Goodwill turned out to be a squat little brick building a short walk from Tully's house. Coo gasped at what was in the big glass windows. Humans? Frozen humans? They stared straight ahead, very still. Their eyes didn't blink.

She pointed, then hid behind Tully.

"Oh. Mannequins!" said Tully. "To show clothes. Weird looking, right?"

Coo soon forgot about the frozen people. There was so much else to look at inside Goodwill. It was like Tully's house, if Tully's house was huge and cluttered with tons of *things*. Piles and piles of fabric everywhere. Worn-looking pieces of furniture. Many cups and spoons and plates, all jumbled in groups together on long metal shelves. Coo sniffed. Goodwill had an unusual smell, too, a bit like very old damp newspapers.

Goodwill

Coo wondered how many humans lived in this place. She looked around, but there was only one other woman wandering among the heaps of stuff.

Tully nudged Coo toward a tall rack of cloth in the back. "These are the kids' clothes," said Tully.

Purple! Pink! Green! Gray! There were sparkles, and puffy things called pompoms, and shirts with words and pictures on them like cartoons. There was shiny fabric and soft dull fabric and very rough heavy fabric, too.

"What do you want, Coo?" asked Tully. "Pick some things out."

Coo couldn't. It was too overwhelming. She plopped down on the fuzzy brown floor and stared at her shoes.

"It's okay, love," Tully said gently. "I'll pick for you."

While Coo watched, Tully scrutinized the different pieces of clothing. Sometimes she made Coo stand and held them up against her body. Finally, when there was a big colorful pile in

Tully's arms, they went to the front of the store where someone helped Tully put them in a bag. Coo sat down in a big brown chair and watched. Then Tully beckoned her, and they went past the frozen people and out the door.

On the way back home from Goodwill, Coo stopped suddenly. Limping down the sidewalk ahead of her, between the snowdrifts and frozen slush puddles and litter, was a small white pigeon.

"Hurt, you?" Coo asked, dropping to a crouch. As soon as the pigeon was at eye level, she saw the piece of glass embedded in her foot.

"Speak, you?" the pigeon gasped. "How?"

"Oh dear," Tully groaned. "Not another hurt bird, not right now."

"Learned from my flock, me," Coo said to the pigeon. "Fix your foot, me. Let me, you?"

Too shocked to resist, the pigeon let Coo take her foot. Coo carefully plucked out the glass and dropped it down a crack in the sidewalk.

"All done, me," said Coo. "Heal now, you."

"My goodness, Coo, good job," Tully said. "Now hurry up and say good-bye to the—"

A sudden rush of pigeons drowned out Tully's voice. Others had heard Coo speak and now they crowded her, asking her questions.

"Speak, you!"

"How, you?"

Unfamiliar birds landed on Coo's shoulders and swooped around her head.

"Learned from my flock, me," she said.

"From the strange flock, she is," said a dappled gray bird. "Roof flock, east."

"Heard of human there," said another pigeon. "Didn't believe it, me."

"Food, you!" Several pigeons at once started asking about food. "Get us food?"

Coo stood up slowly.

"Coo, dear, you were very kind and helped the poor pigeon. Now come along," Tully said, shifting the big sack from Goodwill and grabbing Coo's hand. She dropped her voice to a whisper. "People are starting to stare."

Coo looked up to see dozens of wary humans standing on the sidewalk and peeking out of nearby shop windows, staring at her and the clusters of circling pigeons.

"Go now, me," Coo said to them. "Bye-bye."

She couldn't even see the injured bird anymore, there were so many pigeons. Hooting questions, they followed for a full block as Tully hurried her along.

Pigeon words tumbled around in Coo's mind as they walked up the steps to Tully's building and into the hallway. Meeting the unfamiliar flock made her suddenly miss her own. So much had happened, she'd hardly had time to think about them, but now she felt ill with worry. Were they still hungry? Did everyone make it through the storm?

Coo barely noticed that on the stairs inside the

building sat a small human with a big purple knit hat, black hair, and peculiar glass circles over her eyes.

"Hello, Tully!"

The small human shot up and smiled.

"Oh my goodness. Hello, Aggie." Tully paused, her eyes darting from Coo to Aggie and back again. "What are you doing here?"

"Waiting for Octavia to come down. We're supposed to pick up some stuff for dinner at Food Bazaar."

"How nice. Well, tell your sister hello from me."

A look of confusion passed over the girl's face as Tully opened her door and pushed Coo through.

"Thank you again for my hat, Tully!" Aggie called. "It's so toasty."

Coo peered around Tully and back at Aggie, who looked at her curiously.

"I'm so glad to hear that. Speak soon!" Tully shut the door and then leaned against it, eyes closed.

Coo stared at her. Burr hopped down the

hallway and stuck his head into the Goodwill bag.

"Sorry, Coo," Tully said, sighing and opening her eyes. "I still haven't figured out what I'm going to tell people about you, and it makes me nervous. This is just all so complicated. At least you have proper clothes. Now I need to figure out how to get you to a doctor."

Chapter Nine
Pigeons Leave, Flock Stays

Back at the apartment, Coo carefully went through her new treasures from Goodwill. Tully helped. She gave Coo words: *shirt*, *pants*, *dress*. *Mittens*, *hat*, *boots*.

Best of all, there was a soft, warm, heavy thing, red as a fresh tomato, with a big fluffy hood that nestled around her head.

"A red corduroy coat," said Tully. "I hope it keeps you warm. It just about matches your hat."

For lunch that afternoon, Tully made Coo one of her delicious mud-and-weed sandwiches, which Coo now knew was hummus and sprouts. Afterward she made a drink that was like a warm, chocolate-flavored puddle. Hot chocolate, it was called. It was extraordinary.

Coo's eye kept falling on the slabs on Tully's shelf, the things covered in little newspaper marks. There were no newspapers in Tully's house, but there were these things that seemed almost like them. Tully got a few down and opened one. Pictures of pigeons stared back at Coo.

"I collect books on pigeons. Some of them are more like medical books; they've helped me fix hurt birds," Tully said.

Tully pulled down another book that showed pigeons who looked sick, but quickly put it away.

"This one might be too much for you, Coo. Almost too much for me. I have a bird veterinarian friend, Nicolas. I take the worst cases to him, the ones I can't handle."

Coo opened a book with pages as glossy as glaze frosting.

"Other books are just nice to read and look at," said Tully. "That one is about a special kind of pet pigeon. They're called fancy pigeons."

Coo flipped through the pages. The birds were shaped like pigeons—same bodies, toe-nails, beaks, and eyes—but their feathers were like nothing Coo had ever seen. Wild plumes jutted out from their heads like curling clouds. Thick, white feathers obscured their faces, even their beaks. Bright purple-brown tufts spiked out around their necks. It was like they were wear-ing special pigeon clothing, but when Coo looked closely she saw it was all just feathers. Did some human make special feather suits for them, like Tully knitted slings for Burr? She didn't know how to ask Tully.

"They are bred to look like that. Amazing what feathers can do. They're like the Paris fashion models of the pigeon world, aren't they?" Tully laughed. "Honestly I prefer the humble city pigeon myself. Like Milton here."

Burr hopped over and sat on Tully's lap, happy to get a neck scratch.

Tully didn't call Burr by his real name. She called him Milton.

"Milton?" Coo had asked him the third or fourth time she heard Tully call him that. The word was slightly pigeonish at the beginning, but hard to say at the end. "Burr, you. Milton, no."

"With Tully," Burr said. "Milton, me." He couldn't quite say it either, but got close enough.

Tully brought Coo a dish of pretzels, which she shared with Burr while they paged through the wondrous books all afternoon.

Books were a lot like newspapers. They were wonderful but not totally unfamiliar.

Much more mysterious was the shiny gray box that sat on a shelf near Burr's cage.

"I've been keeping this off when you're awake

because I wasn't sure how you'd react," Tully said the morning after their trip to Goodwill. "But maybe you'll like it."

Tully pressed a black button on a small stick in her hand and the box erupted with loud voices and pictures of people moving just like in real life.

Coo tapped the screen—it was hard as the windowpanes—and stuck her head around the back. Dust bunnies the size of week-old squabs clung to the wires and plastic bits.

"How?" Coo pointed at the television. She was picking up some useful human words.

"It's an image," said Tully. "It was recorded someplace like Hollywood and beamed into the box."

Tully pressed another button. Suddenly the people disappeared, and drawings like the ones Coo knew from newspaper litter danced like they were alive. Tully kept pressing, and a plastic circle glided by itself across a carpet.

"Cartoons and commercials. See? Channels,

Coo. There are lots. Why don't you watch some television? Maybe you can pick up some more English that way."

You were supposed to sit while you watched television, sit for longer than Coo had sat in one place ever except to go to sleep. She did learn new words, but after a few episodes of cartoons she wanted to flap her arms, run around the room, and most of all climb onto the windowsill and look out at the wedge of sky. It was wonderful getting to eat as many sandwiches and pretzels and pancakes as she wanted and to be with Burr. But as the sharpness of her memories of the storm began to wear off in the warmth of Tully's apartment, Coo started to miss the roof.

There were things in Tully's apartment that Coo only noticed as she got more comfortable.

Hanging on the walls, nestled in small windowpanes, were pictures of people. Some were small humans, like Coo. Others were bigger and seemed more like Tully.

Coo had learned that Tully would talk about things she pointed to. Sometimes now the words even made sense.

"Oh, that was me when I was about your age," Tully said when Coo pointed to a small, round girl who stared cautiously out of a black-and-white picture. Coo had been at Tully's house for more than a week. "Tully. Little Tully. Me."

"You?" Coo was shocked. How could Tully have ever looked so different? But when she squinted at the picture, she did see that their eyes were the same.

One picture was of a plump, smiling human with laughing eyes.

"Ben." Tully smiled in a way that was happy and sad at once. "My husband. I wish you could have known him."

"Where?"

"Where is he? Oh, he died, dear." Tully sighed. "I miss him. He would have known what to do with you. He would have figured out how to make everything okay and tell me not to worry so much."

Coo peered at Tully's eyes. They looked strange. Shiny. Almost wet, like rain.

She stepped back in surprise.

Tears. Tully was crying!

Coo touched her own eyes and cheeks. They were dry. Many times on the roof, when she was sad or upset or angry, she had found her eyes and cheeks suddenly burning with tears. Pigeons didn't cry. But it turned out other humans did.

As the days passed, Coo missed the sky and the sound of her flock shifting their wings and chatting more and more. She missed her flock mates.

"Visit the roof, us?" she asked Tully in pigeon one morning.

Tully shook her head. "Can't understand you, dear."

Burr didn't think Coo should return to the roof.

"Human, you," he said. "Stay here, now."

"The flock. Needs us, right?" Coo thought of New Tiktik, Hoop, Pook . . . even Roohoo. What if they had been hurt in the storm? What if they were hungry?

Or what if they were worried about Coo?

"Not worried, them," said Burr. "Pigeons leave, flock stays. Always flock, different pigeons."

Coo stared at Burr. Didn't he miss the others? The roof? The dovecote? Weren't they missing him, and her, at least a tiny bit?

Then she thought back to how the flock had acted when Burr got hurt and went to Tully's. Most of them had stopped talking and wandered away when Coo wondered out loud where Burr was, and if he was all right.

She thought about how it was when she was hungry and needed help. How Ka and the others had made it clear that she should be responsible for getting her own food. They didn't care that she was too weak to even climb down the fire escape.

The memory stabbed sharply, like a stubbed toe. A sudden sharp pain.

But it faded just as quickly. She went back to pestering Burr.

It wasn't wrong to remember and wonder, she was sure of that. After all, Tully had remembered Coo. She remembered her enough to come find her in the storm. Even though they weren't any kind of flock mates at all then.

Pigeons were different. But why? It was troubling.

"Safe here, us," Burr said. "Stay here, us. Flock fine."

Coo didn't agree, but she let it go.

She would find a way to go to the roof, and she would convince Burr to come with her, too.

Chapter Ten
Food Bazaar

Tully bundled Coo into her red corduroy coat and her new boots. She helped her with her hat and mittens. "You've been here more than a week, and I'm running out of food," Tully said. "A trip to the grocery store is in order."

They were going to the roof finally, Coo was sure of it. Somehow Tully had understood her.

Tully hurried her out the door so quickly, Coo didn't have chance to say anything to Burr. Outside, the snow from the blizzard had turned crusty and grayish as stale frosting. Icicles sparkled from the tree branches. It was cold, but the sun was bright, and Coo was warm.

When they reached the end of the street, Coo spotted a metal cylinder on the sidewalk. It was piled high with bags and cups and empty boxes, but crowning the messy tower was something extraordinary: a waxy, brownish-yellow lump.

A *banana*!

Shaking off Tully's hand, Coo grabbed it.

"Coo, no! Put that down. That's trash." Tully snatched the precious banana out of Coo's hand and tossed it over a snowdrift.

Coo yelped.

"Technically that's littering," muttered Tully. "But I'm sure a squirrel will take care of it."

The banana was less than half eaten and only a little bit brown. Coo blinked. She looked at the snow pile into which it had vanished. Then she began to cry.

"Oh dear. Coo, no tears," said Tully. She pulled Coo into a hug, then looked her in the eye. "That was *garbage*. Trash. Bad! You don't need to eat garbage anymore. We're on our way to Food Bazaar. I'll buy you some fresh new bananas, okay?"

Coo nodded, even though she didn't understand why anyone would ever toss away a banana. She felt sad she wouldn't be able to bring it to the others on the roof.

They did not go to the roof.

Tully led her down a few streets and then across a big, flat, tarry place full of cars sparkling in the sun. Tully held Coo's hand very tight. When they reached the front of the building, there were many people milling about, all carrying heavy plastic sacks or pushing silver cages on wheels. Tully held Coo's hand even more firmly and pulled her through a set of glass doors that opened on their own with a *thwack*. Suddenly Coo found herself in a place brighter than the roof on a cloudless day in summer. Lights like hundreds of tiny suns beamed down from the vast ceiling. Objects cluttered her sight wherever she looked. What *was* this place?

"This is Food Bazaar," said Tully. "The grocery store I go to."

Coo blinked in shock. She looked more closely at what was around her.

Great towers of apples. Heaps of lettuces. Hundreds of clumps of green-yellow-brown bananas. Bags and bags and bags of bread. A whole glass case full of perfectly ordered, never-smashed cupcakes with more colors of frosting than she could have imagined. Coo whirled one way and then another. There was this much food in the world? So many hungry days on the roof, when nearby was all this? This was *nothing* like she'd imagined a dumpster to be.

Closest to her was the shelf packed with dozens and dozens of bags of rolls, bagels, muffins, and every other kind of bread. Wiggling her hand out of Tully's, Coo grabbed the first thing she could reach—a sack of cinnamon buns—and tore open the plastic. She stuffed one sweet sugary bun in her mouth and the rest of the bag down her jacket.

"Coo, no! We have to pay for those." Tully reached into Coo's jacket and pulled out the bag of cinnamon buns. She pulled the half-eaten bun from Coo's mouth, too, and frowned.

Coo tried to grab the cinnamon bun back.

"Hush. You're attracting too much attention," Tully whispered. "I'll buy you these and you can eat them later, okay?"

Lots of the humans were stopping to stare. Coo looked down at the shiny cream-colored floor and felt a blush creep up her neck. She didn't like it when other humans stared at her. It wasn't like pigeons staring. Human eyes were so big.

"Let's hurry up. I'll put these in the basket." By the door, Tully had picked up a red plastic box with handles. Into it went the cinnamon buns.

So did some yellow bananas and a bag of bright green lettuce. Then Tully, holding Coo's hand in the tightest grip Coo had yet experienced, led her up and down more aisles brimming with paper boxes, cartons, and bags. One aisle was filled entirely with puffy metallic pillows that crunched and shifted when you squeezed them. "Chips," said Tully, and tossed one in the basket.

"Milk," Tully said when they reached an aisle as cold as snow. "Let's have some ice cream as a treat, too. I'll get Neapolitan, so you can try strawberry, vanilla, and chocolate all at once." Tully opened a foggy glass door and from one of the icy shelves plucked a carton striped with pink, white, and brown. She tossed it into the basket, which was getting very full.

"Food?" Coo said in English, staring in wonder at the things and people all around her. "No birds?"

Why didn't pigeons have grocery stores? It looked so much easier than foraging.

"Only for humans, Coo," said Tully.

"Why?"

128

"Well. Good question. People made grocery stores for themselves. Birds haven't gotten around to that yet. Besides, a lot of this food isn't good for pigeons to eat," said Tully, bracing her basket against a low, open shelf full of bottles while she reached up for some cheese. "They should eat grains and seeds, like corn and barley. Sometimes vegetables are good for them, too, like lettuce."

Tully led Coo over to a part of the store filled with people standing around in lines.

"I can barely carry this basket at this point!" said Tully, setting it down on the floor. "This is where we pay. With money. Because we can't just take whatever we want. First we have to wait for our turn."

It felt strange and uncomfortable to be clustered among so many others. And it was boring. Every time Coo tried to wander away to explore, Tully held her back. Slowly the line inched forward. Eventually Tully lifted up the basket again and began unloading it on the moving black table to their left.

Coo waited. Right at eye level were stacks and stacks of shiny sticks. Coo touched one. It crinkled nicely in her hand. She picked up two. Tully wasn't looking. Coo put the sticks into her pockets, then grabbed more.

"Hey!" shouted a voice. "That kid is stealing candy bars!"

A stranger yanked at Coo's coat. Tully whirled around, eyes flashing. Coo screamed.

"Stop!" Tully shouted. "She doesn't understand."

There was a tussle of hands, humans crowding around, Tully's grasp on her wrist, and someone reaching into Coo's jacket. Coo shut her eyes so tightly she saw bursts of light in the darkness. She threw her hands over her ears and whimpered.

"I'll pay for them." Coo heard Tully's voice, firm and loud, saying words she didn't know. "Let go of her. She's just a small child."

The strange hands came off Coo's coat. She opened her eyes. A tall man in a blue smock scowled at her.

"Ma'am," he said. "You need to make sure your grandchild knows not to steal."

"She knows now," Tully replied. "It won't happen again. We'll pay for them, sir."

Tully stood between Coo and the angry man in the blue smock. Tully's forehead was twisted with wrinkles.

"Coo, we have to pay for the candy bars," Tully said gently. "We can't just take them."

Coo wasn't sure what candy bars were, but she watched Tully put the sticks on the black table, which lurched to life and moved them toward a blue-smocked woman standing behind it. The people who had gathered started to drift away, including the blue-smocked man.

"There," Tully sighed. "Crisis over. And we'll have candy for weeks. But Coo, that was *stealing*. It's very bad. We have to pay for things we want. Watch, I'm giving them money."

Coo pulled her red hat down as far as she could over her head until she could barely see. She looked from the corner of her eye as Tully pulled a stack of green bits of paper from her pocket and handed them over to the woman behind the table. The woman handed back more green paper and some little pieces of metal, and then Tully took the groceries—in plastic bags now, just like the ones Coo wore on the roof—and beckoned for Coo to follow her out of the store.

"I don't know what I'm going to do, Coo," Tully said as they walked over the sparkly, drippy snow-slushed sidewalks toward her apartment. "I might have bitten off more than I can chew with all of this. And these bags are so heavy."

Tully put the bags on a stoop and slowly sank down beside them. The street was deserted. She put her head in her hands so Coo could only see her wool hat.

Coo sat next to her. Food Bazaar had scared her down to her bones, scared her as much as cats and hawks and being alone on the ground. But it was also the most mysterious and wonderful place she'd ever been. Hesitantly, she reached out and touched Tully's hand, mitten to mitten.

"Okay, you?" her head swirling, she asked in pigeon.

"You know I don't understand when you speak like the birds, right?" Tully's face reappeared. She looked sad, but she was smiling. "What a media circus there would be if word got out about you living with pigeons and understanding their speech. Another reason not to bring you to the police; I just know they'd mess it up." Tully took off her mittens, rummaged through one of the bags, and pulled out the open sack of cinnamon buns. "Let's share these," she said, handing one to Coo and taking another for herself.

The cinnamon bun was sweet and rich. It tasted even better on the stoop than it had in the store.

"I like taking care of you, Coo. Since you've come into my life, I'm so happy. After Ben died, I never expected to feel like I had a family again." Tully paused. "But how on earth can I make this work? You're already looking healthier, but I need to figure out how you can go to school. And I need to tell the authorities *something* about you."

Tully's words jumbled in Coo's mind. *Stoop. Happy. Birds.* She understood Tully's tone. Tired, like an old pigeon. Joyful, too. But also scared. If Tully was scared, what did it mean for Coo? Her stomach flipped and flopped.

The roof was safe. Coo could go back to the roof and tell the flock about Food Bazaar. If only they knew! No more dumpsters, no more hunger. They just had to get through the strange doors and avoid the humans in blue smocks. Everything would work out. Coo had been mostly fine there all those years. She could be fine again. Even in winter. She had a coat now, after all.

She looked at the last bit of cinnamon bun in her hand and wondered how far she was from the roof, and if she could get back there right now. She was well enough again to run. But which way?

She wasn't going back without Burr. Somehow

she would have to convince him it was where they belonged, and they would find their way back together.

"You're alive, Tully! Thank God."

Tully and Coo had picked up all the Food Bazaar bags and started the rest of the walk home. They were almost in front of Tully's apartment building when a woman stopped them. She was tall and pale, with bright blue paint on her eyelids and frizzy red hair sticking out from under her purple-and-green hat. Her coat was purple, too, and so were her snow boots. Coo was shocked to see two little smiling orange cat faces dangling from the woman's ears. They weren't real cats, but who would choose to wear things like that? Coo edged back.

"Lucia!" Tully looked up. "My goodness. It's been ages! How are you?"

"Getting over the flu, that's how." Lucia shook her head. The cats danced. "It's bad this year."

"I'm so sorry you were sick," said Tully. "Are you okay now?"

"I'm fine, but goodness, Tully. I've tried you a few times on the phone over the past week with no answer! Did you get a new number? I thought something had happened to *you*."

As Coo watched, Tully turned as pink as strawberry yogurt.

"I—well—I'm so sorry, Lucia. It's not personal. I've been busy taking care of my, um, niece."

"Your niece?"

The woman stared down at Coo. Her lips were very red. The cats seemed to look at Coo too.

Coo stepped behind Tully.

"This is Coo—I mean, Colette. She's called Coo for short."

"*Niece?* Tully, you have a niece?" Lucia's blue-lidded eyes widened. "I thought you were an only child? Ben, too."

"Grandniece, grandniece." Tully adjusted the bags in her hands and nudged Coo in front of her again. "It's complicated. My life has changed a lot."

"A niece. My word! Pleasure to meet you, Coo."

Lucia looked down at Coo while she spoke. She looked at her like no one ever had before, not even Tully. She was smiling, but also seemed to be searching for something.

"How old are you, Colette?" Lucia asked.

Coo stared at her.

"She's eleven," Tully said. "She's nervous around strangers."

"That's smart. You're a lucky girl, Coo, getting to spend time with Tully! Did she knit you that hat?"

Coo looked at Tully, who nodded back nervously.

"Red hat," Coo said. "My hat."

"Unusual accent." Lucia looked puzzled. "I can't place it. Where are you from, Coo?"

"Her parents are—uh—from Eastern Europe," said Tully. "They arrived recently."

Lucia glanced at Tully. "This story gets more

and more interesting. Well. I want to catch up with you! Let's get coffee."

"I would love to catch up with you, too."

"Answer my calls for a start, okay? Don't leave me worrying." Lucia laughed and started to walk down the street. "And good luck, Colette. I hope you have a fun time with your great-aunt."

Coo watched Lucia disappear around the corner. Then she turned to Tully. There was a strange, pinched look on Tully's face.

"Come on, Coo," said Tully after a long silence. "It's cold. Let's hurry inside."

Chapter Eleven
Sick

The morning after the visit to Food Bazaar, Tully pulled a small shoebox down from a kitchen cabinet and put it on the table along with some plain paper.

"I keep this around for when kids in the building come over," said Tully, opening the top. "I can't believe it took me so long to get it out."

Coo peered inside the box. She saw a jumble of colorful sticks. She sniffed. They had a strange smell, sort of dusty.

"Crayons," said Tully. "Markers, too. Here. You can draw." She mimicked scribbling on the paper. "And then we'll work on writing."

Coo picked up a dark purple stick. It felt smooth and cold in her hand. She dragged it across the paper.

A line! A vivid purple line.

Coo gasped.

It was like the rocks she used to scratch shapes and pictures into the grime of the roof, but a thousand times better. She reached into the box and pulled out more crayons. They came in every color—blue, green, pink, brown, black, red. Tully showed her how to pop the caps off the markers and draw with those, too. They made streaks as bright as smashed berries on the paper.

Coo drew and drew and drew. She drew pigeons and dovecotes, bagels and donuts, Tully and Burr. She drew buildings. She drew flowers and trees and fire escapes and hawks. She drew herself.

Burr hopped over and watched. He picked up

a blue crayon in his beak and made a few stubbly dots on the page before dropping it. Coo felt a twinge of sadness. Some things were a lot harder for birds.

Lunchtime came. Tully boiled a package of instant ramen. Coo waited until the soup was cool, then slurped the noodles and salty broth straight from the bowl, still holding crayons and markers in her fists. She didn't want to stop drawing for a moment.

"How about we try writing?" Tully said some time after lunch, as the light grew dim in the room. She switched on the lamps. "I'll show you the alphabet and your name."

Tully pulled out a clean sheet of paper and drew plain, skinny shapes that didn't look like much in particular. While she watched, Coo tapped her foot on the floor, put her head on the table, and spun markers in circles. Writing was not as interesting as drawing.

But then Tully showed her how to spell Coo.

"C-O-O," said Tully, pointing to the shapes she'd just written in black across the top of the paper. "*Coo*. See?"

C-O-O. It was like the marks in the newspapers on the roof, and in Tully's books. And it was her name. Coo sat up and stared.

"B-U-R-R," Tully said, drawing new shapes just below COO. "That's *Burr*. It's shorter than writing out *Milton Burr*." Tully had started calling him by both names.

"Look at this, you," said Coo, turning to Burr where he sat atop the sugar bowl preening his feathers. "It's your name." She pointed to the letters.

"Burr," said Burr. He hopped down and looked closer. "Words, them?"

"Words, them," said Coo. She pointed. "Coo and Burr."

"Us," Burr said, pecking at the letters. "Coo and Burr. Burr and Coo!"

It was like someone had knit together two unfinished pieces in Coo's mind and made a whole. Words were everywhere, and they meant something.

She practiced writing *COO* and *BURR* over and over, filling up page after page, until it was dinnertime and Tully made her stop to eat some spinach lasagna.

A few days later, a weak feeling entered Coo's arms and legs. She sat on the floor playing flock and roof, but the balled-up socks and buttons were suddenly heavy. A few hours later, her throat changed. It hurt to swallow the hummus sandwich Tully made for lunch. After that her head hurt, too, and she lay down on the floor and closed her eyes. Her nose was starting to run. Tully offered to get out the drawing supplies, but Coo wasn't interested.

"Okay, you?" asked Burr, hopping up and down her arm. "Strange, you." His voice fell to a hush. "Beak sick, you?"

"Just tired, me," Coo managed to reply. But she knew it was more than that.

Soon Tully's worried face peered down on her.

"I think you're sick," she said, and pressed her lips together in a thin line. "I may need to bring you to the doctor after all."

Coo burrowed deep as she could into her nest on Tully's floor. *Sick*. A new word. But she knew immediately what it meant. No wonder Tully sounded so upset.

Coo closed her eyes and jerked her head away when Tully reached for her. She knew soon Tully would keep her distance, anyway. As Coo got weaker and snifflier, unable to hide her illness, Tully would ignore her, or maybe even push her out of the apartment. That's what the flock did to sick members—why would Tully be any different?

Coo wondered where she would go. The few times she had been sick before, only Burr had cared for her. He'd brought her bananas and extra donuts, found clean newspaper to wipe her runny nose, and snuggled against her even when she'd burned with fever and all the other pigeons had edged away. Without Burr to help, what would being sick on the roof have been like?

All at once, Coo's hopes about visiting or even living again in her old home shriveled up and vanished. Maybe she could find her way back to Food Bazaar and hide there. Would anyone notice her if she stowed away behind the shelves full of bread? Would they stop her if she only took a little bit of food at a time? Then she remembered the human in the blue apron and his frighteningly strong grip on her shoulders. She shivered. No, not Food Bazaar.

She closed her eyes, burrowed as far down into her nest as she could, and rubbed her drippy nose against one of the blankets. She hoped Tully wouldn't put her out on the street. The only thing to do was wait.

"Soup. You'll need to sit up to eat it."

Coo opened her eyes. Tully knelt beside her

on the floor, hunched over in her tan-and-white sweater so she looked like a big fresh cinnamon bun. She held a bowl with an herby smell. Coo sat up. Her head hurt, and she coughed.

"Minestrone. You can just slurp it. It's a kind of medicine."

Coo looked at the small puddle in the bowl. She'd never encountered a puddle that smelled so good.

"Soup," Tully said again. "Soup!"

"Eat, you," said Burr from his perch on the chair above her.

Coo chugged one bowl, then another, and then a third. *Soup. Sick.* She was learning new human words. But she was learning other things, too. Tully was kind to her, despite her sickness, even kinder than she was when Coo was well. How could that be?

Tully made her bowl after bowl of soup, followed by a cloud-like lump called rice pudding.

She wiped Coo's forehead with cool washcloths.

She gave her a box of the smoothest, softest, plainest bits of newspaper Coo had ever touched and showed her how to blow her snotty nose into them. She added a pile of pillows to Coo's nest and helped her find all the TV programs showing grown-up humans making food—Coo's favorite kind of TV. She moved the television so it was right in front of the nest and then sat next to Coo, doing her best to explain what was on the screen in words Coo understood.

She smiled at Coo, even when Coo's nose was running like a drippy pipe, and she didn't flinch when Coo coughed.

There were some less soothing things Tully did, though. Only the rest of her kindness made Coo tolerate them.

She made Coo hold a plastic stick under her tongue for what felt like ages. When she took it out again, Tully squinted at it, and frowned and sighed, and then said, "It's just a little fever. Not even a hundred degrees. But time for medicine."

What followed was like biting into a good-looking bagel and finding out it had gone moldy. Tully poured candy-purple goop from a bottle into a spoon and motioned for Coo to swallow it. The first taste was sweet, but that sweetness turned bitter, then rancid. Coo screeched and spit it out.

"Cold medicine tastes bad, but it'll help you feel better," said Tully. "Come on, dear."

Burr coaxed her to try again.

"Gave me bad stuff, too, her," he said. "But healed me, it did."

Wrinkling her face, gripping her blanket, Coo managed to swallow down another vile purple spoonful. The broad, relieved smile on Tully's face when she did made the gross taste almost worth it. She did notice that her cough was a little better afterward, too.

Several times a day, Tully pulled a small plastic rectangle out of her pocket and looked at it. Sometimes she flipped it open and punched some of its buttons. Other times she held it against her ear and spoke into it. Sometimes the thing made noise like a car horn. It rattled and honked, and then Tully sighed and said, "Another call," and picked it up and talked into it. She called the thing her cell phone and said that when she spoke into it, there was someone else listening and speaking, too.

It had been a week since Coo fell ill and she was almost fully better. She was sipping hot tea and paging through one of Tully's pigeon books with Burr one afternoon when the cell phone honked.

"Oh gosh," said Tully, looking at it. "It's Lucia. I really should answer."

Lucia. Coo's ears pricked. Something about Lucia made Tully nervous, and that made Coo uneasy.

"Fine, fine," Tully said into the phone. "No, no. Actually, she's staying with me. Just until they get settled here." She paused. "What country? That's complicated, too. Kind of near, um, Estonia."

Tully wedged the phone under her chin and picked up the green-and-white patterned sweater she was making for Coo. She began knitting rapidly.

"Yes, she's my niece," Tully continued. "Honestly, it's so much to explain over the phone. She'll be going back to her family soon. Yes, I'll be very sad."

Tully fell silent again, and her knitting needles began to fly even more furiously.

"Sure, of course I would love to have coffee. This week won't work; Coo is sick at the moment. No, no, not serious, thank God, just a cold. Sorry, Lucia, I have to go. I'll be in touch!"

Tully shut the cell phone and flung it into the fruit bowl.

"Good grief," Tully said, closing her eyes. "After Ben died, I told Lucia about how I was so lonely, with no family left at all. She *knows* we were both only children. And she's a retired social worker; she notices this stuff!" Tully sighed. "I would love to get her advice on how to navigate everything with you, but I'm afraid she'll push me to call the police if I tell her the truth. Why on earth didn't I say I was just babysitting you?"

"Back to family . . . soon?" Coo's heart began to pound. She hadn't understood everything Tully said on the phone, but she understood enough to make her nervous. She let the book slide to the floor.

"Oh, you pick up a lot now, don't you?" Tully raised her eyebrows. "You must be worried." Tully came over to the chair where Coo sat and kneeled next to her. She looked Coo in the eye. "You're staying with me, okay? I'm not sure how I'm going to make this work, but I won't let anyone take you away. I promise. Understand?"

Coo nodded. She hoped she understood, and she hoped it was true.

Chapter Twelve
Aggie

Two days later, when Coo was feeling completely better, there was a knock on the door.

"Into the bedroom," Tully said, shooing Coo through the door. "If it's somehow Lucia, I'm telling her my brand-new pretend family took you back."

But it wasn't Lucia.

"Aggie, what are you doing here?" Coo heard Tully say.

"I'm locked out, Tully," a bright voice answered. "Can I stay with you?"

"Locked out?" Tully said after a pause.

Coo heard the door open.

"Don't you have dance, Aggie?"

"Not doing dance anymore." Aggie's voice sounded sad now.

"Nobody in your family is home?"

"My mom is at *Nutcracker* rehearsal, and Dad is chained to his desk filing some story, and Octavia is in ballet class, and Henry is still at school. And my grandma . . . well, you know."

"What about your friend Julia on the fifth floor? The one who came over with you a few times?"

"She moved out of the city when school started this year."

"Right." Tully sighed. "I forgot about that."

Coo crept out of the bedroom and down the hall.

Aggie stood in the doorway. She wore the same

purple hat and funny glass circles over her eyes as before.

"My dad said if you weren't home, I'd have to wait at the library. I really don't want to. Please, Tully, can I wait in your apartment? I promise not to bug you, or . . . whoever that is." She glanced at Coo and then quickly looked away. "I could do the dishes or something?"

"Of course you don't need to do the dishes." Tully took a deep breath. "And you can wait here, of course. You're always welcome here, Aggie. Come in. This is my niece, Coo. She's staying with me for a while."

How strange it was. Another human sitting at Tully's table! A kid, no less. Aggie plunked herself down in the chair like she lived at Tully's, too. She took a cookie from the plate of them Tully put out and broke it in two. Then she beckoned to Burr.

"Here, Milton! Have you been a good pidge?

Yes, you are such a good pigeon. Do you want some cookie? Yes, you do!"

Milton hopped across the table and right up onto Aggie's arm.

"What a beautiful sling you're wearing today," Aggie said as she held out the cookie for Burr to nibble. "The pink is really nice with your gray feathers. It's been so long since I got to see you! I kept hoping Tully would invite me over like she used to."

Burr let Aggie scratch him under the chin. He tipped back his head and fluffed his feathers. He only did that when he was very happy.

"Would you like some tea, Aggie?" said Tully. "I have Darjeeling, green, mint, chamomile. . . ."

"Mint, please," said Aggie.

"What about you, Coo?"

"Um. Mint."

Mint? Coo was startled at herself. She never chose mint. It was too much like drinking toothpaste. Yet suddenly it seemed like a very interesting kind of tea.

Coo couldn't stop staring at Aggie. Finally Aggie seemed to notice. Frowning, she looked away, and shook her head so her long black hair fell over her cheeks and her eyeglasses.

"I should do my homework," Aggie mumbled. She unzipped the giant pink nylon bag with straps she'd brought with her and began rummaging around in it.

"Maybe you want to color first?" Tully pulled out the shoebox of drawing supplies and smiled.

Aggie paused, her lips drawn together in a straight line.

"Are you too old for that now, Aggie? Sorry, I'm slow on these things."

"No, Tully, don't worry. I'm not too old. I need to make some Christmas cards."

Christmas cards, it turned out, were pieces of paper with drawings on them. You wrote nice messages inside and gave them to people you liked, along with presents. Christmas was a whole day devoted to being nice and sharing. It was next week.

Coo watched Aggie draw small, tidy yellow and red stars all over her paper, along with a green tree and a white bird. The results looked much neater than Coo's wild lines.

"So they don't have Christmas where you're from?"

Coo looked up from her paper, startled. It was the first time Aggie had asked her a question. She glanced at Tully, who had frozen over the teacups, the kettle raised to pour.

"No," said Coo.

"Where *are* you from? You have a funny accent."

Coo looked at her blankly.

"Tully? Where is Coo from?" asked Aggie.

"She's from, uh—Dovecote. I mean, Dovecotia." Tully raised her eyebrows at Coo and shook her head very slightly.

"In the Midwest? But I thought they spoke English there. You're still learning English, right, Coo? I can tell."

"Not Dakota. *Dovecotia*. It's in, um, Eastern Europe." Tully poured the hot water very quickly. "Sugar in yours, Aggie?"

"Extra, please."

Tully nodded and brought the teacups to the table, nestling them in between the rolling crayons and markers. "So, tell me why you decided to drop dance, Aggie," she said, sitting down. "That's a big deal. You loved dance."

"I just decided. That's all. More time to read books."

For a moment, Coo thought she saw Aggie's lip quiver.

"But you didn't want to go to the library this afternoon?" asked Tully.

Aggie focused very intently on the gold heart she was drawing in the corner of her card.

"Of course I'm happy you're here instead," Tully added.

Aggie finished filling in the heart. Then she picked up a green marker and, as Coo studied her, began writing letters in neat, perfect loops on the inside of the card.

"Voilà!" she said, putting down the marker. "It's all done."

Aggie pressed down the crease of the folded paper and then, with a flourish, pushed it up to Burr's beak. "It's for you, Milton. Merry early Christmas!"

"How sweet, Aggie!" said Tully. "Milton will love that. Coo can tell him all about it."

As soon as the words were out of her mouth, Tully's eyes went wide. Puzzled, Aggie looked from Tully to Coo to Burr, and back again. She started to say something, but the doorbell rang. Tully stood and raced down the hall.

"Wonder who that could be," she said nervously, peering through the peephole. "Oh, it's your mother, Aggie."

A tall, thin woman swept through the doorway as Tully opened it. Her ink-black hair was pulled into a tight, perfect bun on her head. She wore a long black coat and a silky red scarf, and she walked with the elegance of a flamingo.

"Thank you so much for taking care of her," Aggie's mother said. "I just managed to get out of rehearsal. How did you forget your keys again, Aggie? Have you thanked Ms. Tully for going to all this effort?"

"Oh, she's thanked me plenty and been a wonderful guest, Vivienne, as always. It was no trouble. Don't worry about it. Coo enjoyed spending time with her."

Aggie's mother's gaze fell on Coo as if she was noticing her for the first time.

"Nice to meet you, Coo. Do you live in the building?"

"She's my niece," said Tully. "Staying with me for a while."

"How nice," said Aggie's mother. "Come on, Aggie, pack up."

Slow as a sleepy pigeon, Aggie began gathering her things.

Aggie

"I just want to say again, I know it's been several weeks, but I'm so sorry about your loss," Tully said, turning to Aggie's mother. "I really miss Isabel's presence in the building. I hope you're all doing okay."

"We're holding up." Aggie's mother dropped her voice to a whisper. "Aggie is taking it the hardest."

"It's very hard to lose a grandmother," Tully said quietly. "Especially one you lived with and who was so kind."

"I'm ready to go, Mom." Aggie stood by the door. "Thank you, Tully. Good-bye, Milton!" She waved to Burr. "Bye, Coo," she said much more quickly, not meeting Coo's eyes. Then she turned and followed her mother out of the apartment.

~ ~ ~

After Aggie left, Tully rummaged around in the closet for a long time. When she emerged, she was holding a plastic tub big enough for Coo to sit in.

"I haven't had any reason to celebrate Christmas for years," she said. "But with you here it's different. And special. After all, in a way this is your very first Christmas."

The top lifted off the tub with a *pop*. Swooping Burr up to her head, Coo peered inside.

It was packed with a jumble of old newspapers. Coo felt a sudden wistful comfort mixed with disappointment. Christmas was about old newspapers?

"It's just a fake little tabletop tree," said Tully, rummaging around in the paper. "My mother must be rolling in her grave. She was a war bride from Germany, and we always had real trees when I was growing up, even when my dad was out of work and we were flat broke. Ben and I switched to plastic, though. Cheaper and better for the environment if you reuse them."

The paper fell away as Tully pulled out a funny little waist-high green shrub and a small bowl that its trunk fit inside perfectly. She sat it atop a table in the main room.

"Outside, inside," said Burr. He gave a branch an experimental nip. "Not food."

"And now the ornaments. Careful, Coo, okay? Some are fragile."

Tully tugged more newspaper out of the tub to reveal tiny beautiful objects, each on a hook or a string. There was an old human with a long beard and a red cloak; a group of perfectly round glass balls in deep, bright colors; a set of silver and gold stars; and a dozen other amazing things, like little birds and hearts and snowflakes.

"Ornaments. Let's hang them on the Christmas tree," said Tully.

With Burr's help—his beak was perfect for picking up the strings—Coo and Tully put the ornaments all over the little tree, until it was glinting with many colors.

"Ack! I forgot the lights! Those are supposed to go on first. Let's see if they still work."

Tully pulled out a long green string covered in tiny bulbs. Together, Burr, Coo, and Tully hung it all over the branches. Then Tully crawled around under the table to the electrical outlet and plugged it in.

Coo gasped. The whole tree was glowing!

"Merry Christmas, Coo." Tully wiped her eyes. "A very merry one indeed."

Coo insisted that Tully keep the tree lit up that night, even after bedtime. She lay in her little nest on the floor staring up in wonder at the way it glowed so warmly.

"Daylight tree," Burr said sleepily. "Never seen, me."

"Special for Christmas, that tree." Coo tried to explain to Burr about Christmas. A whole day humans had to share and give gifts and celebrate mysteries and think about good things.

"Looks sweet," Burr said about the ornaments. "But can't eat."

Pigeons had no holidays at all. It made Coo feel lonely to think about. Pigeons would like Christmas, she was sure of it, if only they knew about it.

Tiny, bright New Tiktik flashed through her mind. The last she'd seen of her was in the blizzard. A cold chill filled her stomach. Was New Tiktik okay? Coo had no way to know. Were the pigeons hungry? She hadn't thought about the flock much while she was sick, but now that she was well again, she felt a sudden anxiousness for them.

"Must see flock, me," she murmured. "Soon."

Chapter Thirteen
Pigeons Should Have a Merry Christmas, Too

"Must visit flock," Coo told Tully the next morning as soon as Tully was awake and shuffling around the kitchen making tea and oatmeal. In the corner the radiator hissed and banged. It was a cold morning. The tree glowed merrily. "Now. Miss them. Miss me. Hungry pigeons, too."

It was a lot to say in human language. Coo felt exhausted afterward. She sat at the table staring at the Christmas tree, then looked back at Tully.

"Please," she added, taking a deep breath. "My family, the pigeons. Christmas now. Family? Hungry family."

"Oh, all right." Tully pursed her lips and wrinkled her brow. "Going back to the alley is such a bad idea, but it hurts me to think of how much you must be worried about them. I'm sure they're worried about you, too. And they probably need food."

"Pigeons should have a Merry Christmas, too," Coo said with great effort.

"True," said Tully. "We can later today. But you must be quiet and listen to me, understand? It's trespassing when we're there. The police could come. It makes me uneasy."

Tully often looked alert when they were outside, her head swiveling to and fro like a hunting hawk. Sometimes she squinted, sighed, and hurried them across the street. For the first time, Coo noticed how many of the shops had green and red

Christmas decorations in their windows.

It was very cold again, and the leftover piles of snow had shrunk and refrozen in hard, spiky, gray drifts.

"You meet so many people when you're a postal worker for thirty years," Tully grumbled, nudging Coo around an icy patch of sidewalk as a woman across the street by the pharmacy waved. "Luckily most of them don't recognize me without my uniform. I'm just not sure I can explain to people over and over who you are without getting us into trouble. Easier to avoid it completely."

It was very hard not to wiggle free of Tully's grasp and dash ahead when they reached the alley. So many days had passed, and now only minutes separated Coo from her flock. She wanted to fly across the busy roads.

Coo thought of running into the police, or Lucia, who she didn't much like, and that helped her slow down. She hopped as she walked and gripped Tully's hand hard. Inside her red coat, safe in the little pouch Tully had sewn for him, Burr muttered and shifted his wings. He had been reluctant to come along, saying he was tired, but Coo had finally convinced him.

Tully pushed the gate open, and they ducked under the chain.

The alley had turned into a small, rippled mountain range of snow. Unlike everywhere else in the neighborhood, nobody had shoveled here. The snow had melted some, but it was still deep.

"Oh dear." Tully sighed. "We're going to have a tough time of it."

Coo knew what trudging through snow was like from her winters on the roof. She didn't care. All she wanted was to see the birds. She plunged ahead, one big, snowy stomp at a time.

At last she turned the corner, and the little hut came into view. Snow capped the bushes and small trees that lined the alley, and frosted the parts of the fences and fire escape that stayed in shade all day. But otherwise it looked the same.

"Flock! Flock! Here, me! Coo!"

"Not so loud! Remember, we aren't supposed to be here," warned Tully.

The beating of many wings drowned out Tully's nervous voice. The flock came rushing down and crowded around Coo, landing on her arms and head and on the ground at her feet. She had forgotten the blissful, safe feeling of being enveloped by feathers, wings, and gentle claws.

"Back, you!"

"Hungry, us!"

"Healthy, you!"

"Gone so long, you!" New Tiktik said. "So worried, me! Hungry, you?"

"No, not hungry, me," Coo said, kneeling close to the ground. New Tiktik landed on her shoulder. "Hungry, *you*? No new dumpster?"

"Long way away," said New Tiktik, hopping back to the ground. "Hungry times, here."

Pigeons cooed all around her. Hoop, nestled close against her neck, peppered her with questions about Tully. Pook interrupted to ask about food. Ka asked about Burr.

"Wait. Surprise for you, me." Coo reached into her jacket and pulled out Burr, plopping him on her other shoulder.

"Burr!" said New Tiktik.

Pigeons shoved one another aside to get closer, rushing at Burr with cooed greetings. Burr hooted happily but shrunk back against Coo's neck.

"Back, flock," Coo said. "Slow, flock."

It was sharp-eyed New Tiktik who noticed first how oddly Burr's left wing hung from his body.

"Wing, Burr!" she said. "Still broken?"

Stunned silence spread through the flock. The birds closest to Coo and Burr edged away. A few abandoned the ground entirely, retreating to the roof of the factory.

Burr turned twice on Coo's shoulder, and then whispered urgently, "Pouch now, me."

Coo felt numb as Burr climbed down into her jacket.

"Fine, Burr is," she said to the other birds. "Can't fly, but lives with me. Happy, he is. Safe. Fine!"

"Can't fly!" the remaining pigeons murmured, shocked.

"Everybody okay?" Tully stood by the hut holding the little brown sack of birdseed. "You look upset, Coo."

Coo couldn't bring herself to explain. How could she have forgotten the way the flock treated sick and injured members? Hoop and the other birds Tully had healed came back cured, or never came back at all.

Tully frowned. "I know I haven't been here in ages, but I've never seen the flock this subdued. Maybe some food will cheer them up."

The flock sailed over to the snow where she scattered the seed, leaving Coo standing alone with Burr who was quiet and still in his pouch.

"What's wrong, Coo?" said Tully when she finished throwing the food.

Human words cluttered Coo's head. She struggled to make order of them.

"Flock is sad," she said finally. "Sad for Burr."

Sad was not the right word at all. But it would do.

"Tell them Burr will be just fine. He's safe with us. Aren't they happy to see you after all this time?"

Coo had planned to tell the pigeons all about Christmas. She'd even wondered if they could come over to Tully's house to see the tree and celebrate together. But the way they treated Burr made all those thoughts vanish.

Plump purple Roohoo landed on Coo's head.

"Broken wing, Burr?" he said. "Show me, you."

Of course Roohoo would be the one to come pester Burr. Coo was wary.

"No, Roohoo. Go eat, you," said Coo, pushing him off.

Her time with humans had made her bolder in dealing with him. Roohoo took off from her head and landed on her shoulder.

She shooed him off again.

"Stop, you," Burr said to her. He wiggled his head out toward Roohoo, then hopped onto Coo's other shoulder.

"Seem okay, you." Roohoo leaned around Coo's neck and nudged Burr's wing with his beak. "First healed broken wing seen, me. Hurt much?"

"No," said Burr. "Sling helps."

"Sling?" Roohoo nipped at the pink and white yarn. "Strange bird, you."

"Christmas now, Roohoo. Heard of it, you? Human day for being nice," Coo grumbled. "Be nice!"

"Humans? Nice? Killing flocks, them."

"What?" said Coo.

"Heard rumors, me," said Roohoo. "Flocks at the new dumpster said. Lots of pigeons dying."

"Beak sick?" Coo shrank back, pulling Burr off her shoulder and tucking him back down into his pouch. She remembered her own illness last month. What if her flock got sick? Or Burr? Would Tully be able to help them?

"Not beak sick. Human sick. Bad seed, maybe."

"Hush, Roohoo." Old Tiktik landed on Coo's head. "Just rumors. Sick, no flocks we know."

"Yet," Roohoo snapped. He took off and zoomed up toward the roof.

Coo was very quiet on the walk back to Tully's apartment. Worries swirled through her mind. Burr dozed in his pouch. Dusk fell. The sky was turning gray and purple. The bright holiday lights in the shops looked suddenly silly. Why did humans bother with holidays?

"Did it make you feel funny seeing them?" asked Tully. "You seem down."

Coo hugged herself. She felt Burr shift under her coat. At least they always had each other. She felt a pang of guilt for bringing him to the alley.

"Need to go back soon," Coo said, her worries for the flock overtaking her disappointment in how they had treated Burr. "Flock is hungry."

"Can't they look for more food on their own?"

Tully sighed. "I want to help, but it makes me nervous going there."

"Very hungry. We go back soon? Important, Tully."

Every day she was able to say more and more in human language. She was about to tell Tully what Roohoo had said about other flocks falling ill when Tully hushed her.

"Oh, what luck." Tully's voice was suddenly sharp and quiet. "Coo, don't say anything."

"Tully! Merry Christmas!"

Standing in front of them, barely recognizable in a great swath of scarves and her long purple coat, stood Lucia. She was holding a bunch of Food Bazaar bags, and Tully seemed to wince when Lucia plopped them down on the sidewalk.

"Merry Christmas, Lucia," Tully said. "How's it going?"

"Too cold for me." Lucia pushed her scarves around until more of her face popped out.

Coo noticed her eyelids were somehow lime green this time, but she was relieved to see there were no cats hanging from her ears. Instead there were tiny dark green cars—not much better, when Coo thought about it.

"Now that I'm retired, I don't know why I don't move somewhere warm. I'm ready to be done with blizzards and winter," Lucia said. "A question for another day. More important—how are *you*, Coo?" She smiled down at her. "Excited for Christmas? Still staying with your . . . aunt?"

Coo stared at Lucia. Tully nudged her, and she slowly nodded.

"Tully, you have to tell me this story! I'm dying to know. So you found a long-lost sister from somewhere in Europe, and she left her granddaughter with you?"

"Oh, it's such an interesting story but we're running late for an . . . appointment."

"Of course, of course. When can we meet up? How much longer is Coo staying with you?"

"At least a few weeks."

"She's not spending the holidays with her family?"

"We're going to celebrate here," said Tully.

"Wonderful! Wait—oh my—what is *that*?" Lucia shrieked. The cars hanging from her ears jumped.

Confused by how long they'd been standing still, Burr had managed to wiggle himself to the top of his pouch and stick his head out from Coo's coat.

Lucia was so shocked she stumbled backward, nearly tripping over her groceries. Tully caught her arm just in time.

"Burr," said Coo. "My pigeon." She helped him up onto her shoulder.

"I rescued him this fall," said Tully. "He has a broken wing, so he'll live with me forever now. Coo really took a shine to him."

"Good grief." Lucia stared at Burr warily. "I forgot about all your pigeon stuff. Are you sure it's safe having a wild animal in the house?"

"Of course it's safe."

"He doesn't have . . . diseases?"

Coo studied Lucia. She could tell Lucia didn't like Burr.

"Burr is a good pigeon," Coo said.

"I'm sure he is," Lucia said, smiling faintly. She picked up her grocery bags and started walking down the street. "Call me, Tully!"

"Oh, what a mess!" Tully said when they got home. She helped Coo out of her coat, then went to the kitchen and started making grilled cheese for dinner. Burr settled down to nap in his cage.

"I love Lucia, but why oh why, of all the people, do we keep running into her?" Tully said, getting the bright orange cheddar out of the fridge. "Luckily it seems Burr scared her off. I'm just concerned she'll keep asking questions I don't want to answer. Even though I really do need some of the answers she could give *me*."

Very little of what Tully said made sense, but Coo

understood her anguish. Coo's troubled thoughts about the flock vanished. Gently, hesitantly, she rested a hand on Tully's arm.

"Everything is okay," Coo said, as clearly as she could. "Fine here. Tully and Coo."

Tully smiled at her, but it was a smile that looked almost like crying.

"It makes me so happy when you speak, Coo. I wish everything *was* okay. But Lucia knows Ben and I didn't have any siblings. That means we can't have had any nieces—or grandnieces. Do you understand?" Tully got out a pan, turned on the stove top, and started slicing cheese.

Coo nodded, though she was unsure. Humans had so many words for family. Pigeons just had flock mates.

"She used to be a social worker. She worked for child protective services for years. I don't think she'd turn me in, but I don't know what to tell her." Tully paused. "I should tell you it's a possibility. If the state looked into things, they might take you away."

"Away where? Back to roof?"

"No. Somewhere else they would consider safe. Without me, or your flock, or Burr."

"How?" Coo's stomach flipped. "Tell them no. I stay with you."

Slowly Tully began to explain to Coo about things called government, laws, and rules. About humans who made decisions about other humans, about where they could live and who they could be with. "The authorities," she called them.

It was bewildering, but as Tully spoke, Coo understood more and more. Coo's hands turned clammy. All along she had assumed Tully was the strongest and most important human in the world. But apparently, this was not so.

"Remember the other people I brought with me to find you, before you came to live with me?" Tully gestured for Coo to sit down. The grilled cheese was ready. "The day you hid in the bush and a cat ran out. I knew you were in there, even though they acted like I was nuts."

With a jolt, Coo remembered. The clanking metal. The crackling boxes. The blue clothing. The loud voices.

"The police," said Tully. "They also do good things. They protect people. But if they think you are doing something wrong, they stop you."

"Wrong, me here with you?"

"No. It's not wrong. But I have made a lot of mistakes trying to keep you. It's my fault." Tully sat down across from Coo and sighed. "The police, other authorities, social workers like Lucia . . . they would think it's a problem. Because it's not official. And for other reasons. You should eat, Coo. Your sandwich will get cold."

But Coo wasn't hungry. "Other reasons?" she asked. "What are other reasons?"

"Well, they need to check that you aren't a missing child. I looked at lists of missing children on the computer at the library after I met you, and I didn't see any that seemed likely to be you, but who knows? It does trouble me." Tully frowned. Coo noticed she wasn't eating her own sandwich, either. "And there's the fact you haven't seen a doctor."

"Doctor?"

"People who help people who have been sick. And also help you so you don't get sick in the first place. You've been gaining weight so fast I haven't been as worried, but I need to make an appointment eventually. Doctors are good, but I'm worried if anyone found out how you were raised by pigeons, there would be such a circus—you'd become the Bird Girl; everyone would want to study you," said Tully. "You wouldn't have a normal life."

Tully tried to explain, but Coo could no longer listen or make sense of what Tully said. All Coo heard was that she might have to go somewhere else, somewhere that was not Tully's apartment or the roof. Her heart was pounding. She pushed the sandwich away. Grabbing a sack of Food Bazaar cinnamon buns from the counter, she dove into the deepest part of her nest and shut her eyes.

"Okay, you?" Burr asked, hobbling out of his cage.

"Humans," Coo whispered. "Scary."

"Tully?"

"No. Other humans." Coo thought about Roohoo's dark warnings. "Humans do bad things to humans, too."

"Some humans, bad," said Burr. "More humans, good. Understand, you?"

"Understand, me," Coo said in a very small voice.

She pulled out a cinnamon bun and slowly began to eat it, sharing it with Burr. He let her have all the raisins.

"No worries, you," Burr said, pushing another raisin in her direction with his beak. "Together, us. Always."

Tully sat down on the floor and scooted up to Coo's nest. "Can I have one of those cinnamon buns?" she asked.

Coo handed Tully the sack.

"Thanks," said Tully. She rummaged around and took out a slightly squished bun. "I know it's scary. I promise I'll do everything I can to protect you. I'm going to figure out a plan for talking to the authorities. Maybe Lucia can help me. I don't want you to worry, okay?"

Coo nodded.

"Good. For now, let's eat and enjoy the holidays."

Chapter Fourteen
A Christmas Card

Most mornings Coo woke up when it was still dark, just like a bird, long before Tully. Usually she lay quietly in her nest with a lamp on, looking at books. But on Christmas morning she crept to the shelf where Tully kept her box of art supplies and carefully took it down.

"Doing what, you?"

Burr came over and pecked at the marker in her hand.

"Drawing a card, me." She thought again about how to explain Christmas in pigeon. "Remember? Sharing day today, for humans. Show love with a paper. And gift."

Coo didn't have a gift for Tully. She had spent all week thinking of what she could possibly get or make for her without Tully knowing, and finally gave up. A card would have to do.

Burr wandered off while Coo continued drawing hearts and stars all over the paper, dozens and dozens of hearts and stars, until she had filled every inch. Then she carefully placed the card on the table and waited for Tully to wake up.

"For me? Really?" Tully stood by the table in her bathrobe, as fluffy and pink as a dawn cloud, staring at Coo's card. "Thank you."

Coo watched Tully's face. Tully's lips pressed together. Then they trembled. Her eyes got wet.

Why was Tully crying?

"You don't like it, Tully?"

"Oh, Coo." Tully put down the card and wiped her eyes. Then she smiled. "No, I love it."

"Crying?"

"Because—well, because I am thinking of Ben and how much he would have loved to know you. We always wanted a child. I just wish he could be here now. Merry Christmas, dear."

Coo looked at the photo of Ben. It hung on the wall above the Christmas tree. His happy eyes seemed to meet hers.

Burr, with the knack he always had for moods, even when he didn't have the words to explain them, hobbled up onto Tully's shoulder.

Tully looked at the card again and then back at Coo. "I was supposed to get up first, you know!" she said. "I was going to put some presents under the tree. Technically Santa Claus should have come with them, but we didn't get a chance to send him a letter."

Coo knew who Santa Claus was. There was a heavily bearded man dressed in a red suit who sat outside Food Bazaar and posed for pictures with people. Tully had explained about Santa and presents, and that the Food Bazaar Santa wasn't the real one. The real one lived at the North Pole and flew—flew!—around the world with his team of reindeer, visiting houses by climbing down the chimneys. "Or through windows and fire escapes, here in the city," Tully had added.

Coo wasn't sure how she felt about a strange man in a red suit appearing through the window, but she liked the idea of presents. And flying.

From a high cabinet shelf in the kitchen Tully pulled down three bundles wrapped in gold and green paper.

"Here," said Tully. "These are for you."

Coo stared at them for a while. They were very beautiful. Then she began tearing them open. Burr helped—he loved ripping paper with his beak.

The first gift was a book. On the front cover was a picture of a girl flying with a goose. Inside was all words, no pictures.

"*The Fledgling*," Tully said. "I thought it looked good, right? We'll read it together."

The second package was a mysterious bundle of small knitted sweaters, dresses, and pants. There was even a tiny pair of felted shoes. The clothes were too small for Coo, but too big for Burr. Coo stared at them, puzzled.

"Open the third package," said Tully, beaming.

The last package was bigger and bulkier than the other two. Coo tore away the paper. Her eyes widened. Staring up at her was a small human. She had blond hair, just like Coo, but her hair was yarn. The clothes were exactly the right size for her.

"A doll," said Tully. "I made her, too, like the clothes, very quietly at night. I was so afraid you'd wake up!"

Coo stared down at the doll in wonder. The doll stared back. She was smiling.

"Mine?"

"All yours. You need to give her a name."

A name. Coo thought and thought. She didn't know many human names.

"Queens," she said finally, thinking of a word she'd seen written out on many signs around where Tully lived, and which Tully had helped her sound out.

"Hmm. Lovely!" said Tully. "How about Queenie as a nickname?"

Queenie. That felt nice to say.

Coo hugged Queenie and then carefully dressed her.

Christmas was magical indeed.

They were returning from a special Christmas lunch at Jade Moon Kitchen when Coo noticed a piece of paper sticking out from under Tully's door. She reached down and grabbed it.

"What's that?" said Tully, her voice sharp.

Tully glanced over her shoulder. Coo did, too. The hallway was empty.

"Can I see it? Oh, it's for you, Coo." Tully

relaxed and unlocked the door. "I think I know who it's from."

Coo ripped the sealed envelope. More paper—green and red and covered in gold glitter that flaked onto her hands.

"A Christmas card!" Coo whispered. She opened it. Inside was writing. Her reading lessons with Tully were just beginning to get less frustrating—but suddenly it was all too overwhelming. She clutched Queenie to her chest, unable to make out a single letter. "Read it, Tully!"

"Of course, sweetie."

Dear Coo,

Merry Christmas! I liked drawing with you. It is fun you get to live with a pigeon. They are the coolest birds.

Have a good Christmas.

Sincerely,

Aggie

Coo sat in stunned silence. She picked up the card and studied every inch of it. Then she asked Tully to read it twice more.

"See how nice it is to get a Christmas card?" Tully asked, smiling.

Coo carefully placed the card on the table. Burr came over and pecked up a piece of glitter. "I need to make one for Aggie," she said. "Right now."

Coo's card was not as neat as Aggie's, and Tully had no glitter in her box of supplies. Tully offered to write a message inside the card, but Coo didn't like that idea, so instead Tully spelled out the letters, slowly, as Coo shaped them with her marker:

TO AGGIE
FROM COO

"Coo!" Burr said happily, when she finished the last O. He was quite good at recognizing some words.

Drawing and writing had taken a long time. It was dark outside when Coo gingerly stuffed the card into an envelope Tully dug out of the junk drawer. Burr hopped into his cage to go to sleep. Coo grabbed Queenie and tucked her under her arm.

It was odd to leave the apartment without a coat or hat or scarf. It was even stranger to walk up the stairs Coo had seen every day for months but never climbed. They were dark brown and chilly and had cobwebs in their corners. Coo gave Queenie a squeeze.

Tully led them up three whole floors and stopped outside a gray door labeled 4C. On either side of the door was a jumble of shoes, umbrellas, and scooters. The hallway smelled like chocolate and peppermint.

"Let's just slip the card under the door," Tully said. "It's suppertime and we shouldn't bother them."

Coo wedged the card underneath and stepped back.

They were already starting down the first flight of stairs when 4C's door popped open behind them.

"Wait!" a voice called.

Aggie stood in the buttery yellow light spilling out into the hall from her home. She wore neon-pink pajamas and a pair of fuzzy green socks and nudged her glasses up her nose as she peered down the stairs.

"Coo, wait!" she said.

Hesitantly, noticing the uncomfortable look on Tully's face, Coo went back up the steps.

"Thank you for the card," said Aggie. The warm chocolate scent wafted around her. "Do you want to come hang out for a bit? My sister just made peppermint brownies."

A plump, sleepy-looking man with large glasses appeared behind her.

"Is that okay, Dad?" Aggie asked, turning to him. "Can Coo come over and have a brownie?"

"Sure. Are you a new neighbor, Coo?"

"Coo is my niece," Tully said, stepping up from the stairway. "Hi, Phil. Merry Christmas."

"Oh, Merry Christmas to you, too, Tully. Sorry I didn't see you there," said Phil, blinking. Coo noticed he was wearing pajamas printed all over with small cartoon dogs reading newspapers. "Long day. I was up at four this morning covering that giant steam explosion in Midtown."

"Oh my goodness." Tully's eyes widened. "That sounds terrible."

"Yeah, it blasted a huge crater in the street," said Aggie's dad.

"No injuries!" Aggie said brightly. "Just some parked cars that fell in the hole. The best kind of exciting disaster, right, Dad?"

"Right, except for the part where I hauled myself to midtown before dawn on Christmas Day," said her dad, frowning. "That was truly tragic."

"Well, Coo and I definitely don't want to bother you—"

"No, Tully, it's completely fine," Aggie's dad

said, yawning. "Come in, Coo. If it's okay with you, Tully."

"Yes!" said Aggie, pumping her fists into the air. "Tully, is it okay?"

Coo looked from Aggie to Phil to Tully. Aggie's face was eager and shy. Her dad's was tired. Tully's was nervous—her lips were set in a tight line and her eyes looked small. But when Coo met her gaze, she sighed and nodded.

"I'll be back up to fetch you in thirty minutes, Coo. Just come down if you need me. And be polite and take your shoes off, Coo; Aggie's family doesn't wear shoes in the house."

Coo balanced Queenie on her knee while she ripped the Velcro off her sneakers. Tully turned and went down the stairs. When Coo looked up, Tully was gone. Clutching Queenie, Coo walked into Aggie's apartment alone.

Chapter Fifteen
Aggie's Apartment

Aggie's apartment was so different from Tully's!

Pictures crowded the cream-colored walls—paintings, drawings, posters, and photographs of buildings, animals, birds, and people. Coo looked closely at one photo of a woman in a poofy skirt and strange shoes holding her arms up in the air in an arc and, startled, recognized Aggie's mother.

"My mom was a principal in a big ballet

company," said Aggie. "Now she teaches and does choreography and stuff."

Coo nodded, even though she didn't know what *principal*, *choreography*, or *ballet* were.

They went to a kitchen crowded with dishes and tangled potted plants, and Aggie carefully cut two brownies from a fragrant tray balanced on pans atop the stove. She plunked them on a pair of small plates.

"Are you into playing with dolls?" said Aggie, looking at Queenie.

Coo hesitated, not quite understanding, then nodded. "Her name is Queenie. Tully made her."

"Tully made that doll? Like, sewed it and everything?" Aggie raised her eyebrows. "That's so cool."

Plates of brownies in hand, Aggie led Coo out of the kitchen and through a room cozily packed with sofas and chairs and tables. She turned down a hallway lined with bookshelves, almost as many as at the library where Tully had taken Coo a few times. Through a slightly opened door, Coo saw an older girl laying on a bed piled with pillows, reading a book. From underneath another door came the sound of a guitar.

"My older brother and sister," Aggie said. "They don't really play with me much anymore. Teenagers, you know."

"Oh," said Coo. She didn't know, but she also didn't want to tell Aggie that.

They were halfway down the hallway when Coo froze. Stalking its way toward them, white, fluffy, and ferocious, was something she never expected to see indoors. She gasped, hugged Queenie, and pressed herself against the wall.

"Don't be scared, Coo! It's just Sugarplum. He's a sweetie."

While Coo watched in horror, Aggie put the brownie plates down on some books and swooped the cat into her arms. She nuzzled its neck. The cat went limp and swished its tail.

"Want to pet him?" Aggie asked. "Seriously, he won't bite or scratch."

Hesitantly Coo touched the cat's back. His fur was as soft as Tully's thickest alpaca yarn. To Coo's shock, he made a low growl and his whole body seemed to vibrate. She snatched her hand back.

"See, he's purring," said Aggie. "He likes you. He's a good cat. Popo always said he was 'less trouble than a cushion'! He was really my grandma's cat."

Aggie gave Sugarplum a squeeze then let him down. Coo thought she saw something sad ripple across Aggie's face.

Sugarplum scampered down the hallway and disappeared.

"Here's my room." Aggie handed one brownie plate to Coo. She picked up her plate and then the brownie, and took a bite. Then she opened the last door in the hall. "My parents turned the dining room into their room so we could each have our own."

It was a very small room, only slightly bigger than the dovecote. Aggie's bed took up most of it. On the floor was a soft pink rug that hugged Coo's feet like a pile of feathers. On the walls were posters of girls and women in the same outfits Aggie's mother wore in the picture of her in the hallway. Perched on a high shelf above the bed was a row of dolls, much fancier ones than Queenie, looking still and sleepy. All around on the floor, and peeking out from underneath the dresser wedged in by the door, were piles and piles of books.

Coo took a nibble of her brownie. Then another and another. It tasted like a peppermint candy and a chocolate bar and a piece of cake, all rolled into one. It was delicious. She fed one large crumb to Queenie, then popped it into her own mouth when Queenie was done.

"We could draw if you want," Aggie said, finishing the last bites of her own brownie. "I have a lot more art supplies than Tully."

Aggie pulled a large, flat, plastic tub out from under

her bed. Coo gasped at what was inside. Hundreds
of crayons in every color. Dozens of markers, thick
and thin. A rainbow of paper. Jars of glitter. Stacks
of stickers. She stared at it all, speechless.

"It's okay if you don't want to," Aggie said. She
quickly covered the tub again. "We could—"

"No! Draw, please."

They drew in silence at first. Coo was making a
pigeon using markers in three shades of gray. She
glanced at Aggie's drawing. It was a girl standing
on one foot, with the other in the air.

"What's that?" Coo asked.

"A dancer. A ballerina."

"What's a ballerina?"

"A ballerina is a ballet dancer. You don't know
what ballet is?" Aggie looked puzzled.

Coo focused on coloring a wing. She was trying
hard not to blush.

"Where did you say you were from again?
Duv . . . duv something?"

"Dovecotia."

"Oh right," said Aggie. "Never heard of it. What language do they speak there?"

"Bird."

"Weird. Never heard of that, either. But I'm not good at paying attention in school, so there you have it." She paused. "Not good at dance, either. They made me stop."

"Stop dancing?"

"Yeah."

Coo knew what dance was. She'd loved to twirl, leap, and move, especially when she heard music, and Tully had told her the word for it.

"I was in a really important ballet school since I was little. But they make you audition and last summer . . ." Aggie looked down. "I didn't get asked back."

Ballet, it seemed, had something to do with dance.

"Why?" said Coo. "Just go back."

"That's not how it works. They have to want you, and they didn't want me."

"Why?"

Aggie pressed her lips together so tightly they disappeared.

"Because I'm not good enough."

"Not good?" Coo was baffled. Anyone could jump and spin.

"I can't dance! I'm bad!"

Coo looked at Aggie carefully. She had pretty, glossy black hair, a round face, and blue plastic glasses. Coo peeked at Aggie's feet. Were they injured in some way she hadn't noticed before? No. They looked fine. "But you love dancing," Coo said. "That makes you good."

Aggie looked at her with eyes that were so full of hurt, Coo flinched. She knew she had said something wrong, but what?

"No, it doesn't. Other girls were better. So the teachers didn't let me come back. No more ballet."

"Do ballet anyway!" Coo said. "Why stop?"

"It's not the same without classes." Aggie stretched out her legs and studied them, frowning.

"You need lessons and other people to dance with, or it's not ballet."

"No sense, ballet."

Aggie looked up. "You've never seen ballet, have you?"

Coo shook her head.

"Okay. Well, see the dancers on my posters there? They're ballerinas."

She pointed to a trio of women in tight pink tops, puffy skirts, and strange shoes. Their hair sat atop their heads in perfect, shiny buns, and they looked very serious.

"They dance with really beautiful costumes on a big stage," said Aggie. "It's the most amazing thing to watch."

"You like doing ballet?" asked Coo. "Why?"

"You mean instead of just watching?" Aggie looked surprised. "Watching is good, I guess. But when you actually dance, it's like—it feels like everything is magical, instead of normal. Like you go to another world." She lifted up her arms. "Like

I'm maybe flying, even though my feet are on the ground."

Coo raised her eyebrows. She knew what it felt like to want to fly.

"Show me ballet, Aggie?"

"Right now?"

"Please?"

"It won't look right in pajamas." Aggie scrunched up her mouth and nose. "And it's really crowded in here. Also, I'm not good."

Coo didn't care about any of that, and with a reluctant sigh, Aggie stood up.

"See, this is first position, and second," Aggie said, quickly moving her feet into shapes Coo never thought about feet making. "And here's fifth."

Coo was puzzled. She thought dance meant moving, not standing still in funny ways. Maybe ballet was different than she'd imagined.

"And this is a plié, and a pirouette—"

Aggie stopped speaking. She was just moving. Her arms arced up and her legs leaped and her body twirled. Coo watched, mesmerized. No wonder Aggie was so sad. Ballet *was* magical!

"Can you teach me?"

Aggie froze mid-plié and looked at Coo.

"Me? Teach *you*?"

Coo blushed.

"Yes! Stand up! We'll start with the first position."

Aggie's dad poked his head around the door. "Time to go, Coo. Your aunt is here. Aggie, it's getting close to bedtime," he said.

Coo didn't want to leave, but she knew she had to. She brushed the brownie crumbs off Queenie and onto the plate and stood up.

"You can have my drawing," Coo said to Aggie as they left the room.

"Thanks," said Aggie. She was walking very slowly down the hallway.

Coo followed, clutching Queenie and keeping one eye peeled for Sugarplum.

"You're so lucky to have Milton," Aggie

continued. She stopped to pick up a book from the floor and shove it into a gap on the shelves. She looked back at Coo. "Pigeons are cool, cooler than parakeets or parrots or even owls, at least in my opinion. They're so smart, but nobody really notices." Aggie got a dreamy look. "Did you know pigeons can read letters? Like, they know the alphabet, if people show them. They even can tell when words have a typo. Scientists did an experiment and proved it. I saw it on TV."

"Yeah. Milton Burr knows my name," Coo said. "He reads words."

"Really?" Aggie raised her eyebrows. She leaned against the bookshelves. "How do you know?"

"I . . . know." Coo bit her lip. She wasn't sure how much it was okay to tell Aggie. Somehow Coo knew Tully would be upset if Aggie learned that Coo could speak to birds, and understand them, and had lived with them for so long. "Teach me more dance?" Coo said, hoping Aggie wouldn't ask more questions.

"Yeah, let's do it! This weekend?"

Coo nodded.

Aggie beamed.

"They made Aggie stop ballet," Coo said that evening as she and Tully ate a dinner of tofu scramble. "But she loves doing ballet."

Burr sat at Coo's elbow, pecking at a dish of oyster crackers. Queenie was propped up against a glass of water, smiling happily at the ceiling.

"Her parents? Really?" asked Tully. "I would think her mother would want her to do ballet."

"No. Teachers."

"Oh dear. I know the school she was in was very competitive."

"They said she was bad."

"I hope they weren't that blunt. Poor Aggie." Tully sighed. "I thought she was just sad because her grandmother died, but she has other things going on. I'm sure she misses her friend Julia and her friends from ballet, too."

"Aggie showed me ballet. She loves dancing. Why would they make her stop?"

Coo thought of the flock. Some pigeons were faster and more graceful in the air, but nobody ever made the slower ones stop flying.

"Ballet gets very serious as you get older," said Tully. "And competitive. Competitive means everyone fighting for a spot."

Coo remembered the way Aggie twirled and leaped and swooped around her small room. It didn't seem like it should be serious or competitive.

"You didn't tell her about your—well, where you lived before, right?" Tully asked. A look of worry passed over her face. "About the pigeons and how you came to live here."

"No."

"I'm sorry to ask you to keep secrets, but it's safer that way. I don't want to think what would happen if Aggie's father starts asking questions. He's a newspaper reporter." Tully closed her eyes and winced. "I should have said you were from Estonia or something, not a fake country like Dovecotia. I wasn't thinking. You understand, right, Coo?"

Coo nodded. She did understand. Mostly. But not completely. It was hard to find the words to ask more questions.

"Confusing, being human," she said to Burr, refilling his dish of oyster crackers.

"Good food, humans have," said Burr. "Confusing, how?"

Coo sighed. It was getting harder to explain things in pigeon, too.

Chapter Sixteen
Feeding Pigeons Is Not Illegal, Sir!

After Christmas, Aggie came over as often as she could. As often as she could turned out to be every day. School was on break for the holiday.

"Octavia and Henry are supposed to be keeping an eye on me," she explained to Tully and Coo. "But they'd much rather I stayed out of their hair."

While Tully knit and cooked or did paperwork and ran errands, Aggie and Coo took over the living room. But it wasn't a living room anymore:

it was a theater. They were performing ballets, though Aggie insisted they weren't real ballets, because the steps weren't right.

Coo insisted it didn't matter.

"Dance like *this*," Coo said on the third day Aggie came over, jumping in the air and touching both her toes. "Real ballet? Don't care."

Aggie had been trying to teach her about a ballet called *Swan Lake*, but Coo wasn't very interested. She had another idea for a ballet.

"*Pigeon Roof*," Coo said. Human words were coming faster and faster to her. "About a girl who lives with a flock of pigeons on a roof. Then a pigeon gets hurt by a hawk, and she has to save him and goes to live with humans."

Tully's clacking knitting needles went silent.

"Oops," Coo whispered.

Aggie didn't seem to notice anything weird. "I know Balanchine made up a lot of new ballets. I guess we could, too. But honestly it sounds more like modern dance, not ballet."

"Hawk, me," said Coo. "You dance, and I catch you."

"Okay. But let me show you a chassé step first. It's like a hop. You can swoop like a hawk doing that. Like this . . ."

A few days after Christmas, Coo managed to convince Tully to go back to the alley with more food for the hungry flock.

"All right, all right, I don't want to be responsible for a pigeon famine." Tully sighed as they ate oatmeal with honey and pecans. "But you're going to stay here with Aggie, got it? Her sister and brother can watch you for a bit."

"No," said Coo. "I will come with you. Aggie, too."

"Absolutely not. Can you imagine what her parents would say?"

Coo couldn't. Aggie's parents were mysterious figures, rarely home and barely aware, it seemed, of what Aggie did most days.

~ ~ ~

"You can't go without me!" Aggie exclaimed later that morning after Coo explained to her about the hungry pigeons who needed to be fed. "I want to meet the flock Burr came from."

Coo longed to say it was the flock *she* came from, too, but she was careful not to break Tully's rule. Especially with Tully cleaning up from breakfast just a few feet away.

"Aggie, I don't think your parents would be okay with that," Tully said, clearing her throat. "It's beyond Food Bazaar, near the rail yard."

"No problem. I'll ask!" Aggie leaped up. "My mom is home today, actually."

Five minutes later Aggie was back. She was holding a clear bag of sliced bread and beaming.

"Not only did my mom say yes, she gave me this old bread for the birds. She says hi, Tully."

"Hooray!" shouted Coo. "Let's go."

Tully put down her dish towel and sighed.

~ ~ ~

"I wish winter break was a month long. Two months!" Aggie said as they waited to cross the busy road between Tully's neighborhood and the rail yard.

It was a warm winter day and most of the snow had melted. Everything was wet, and the cars and signs and even the sidewalks were dazzling in the bright sun. Coo wished Queenie and Burr were with her so she could show them how clean and brilliant everything was, but Tully had made her leave both at home.

"What school are you going to, Coo?" asked Aggie.

"Our turn!" Tully said brightly, grabbing both their hands. "Must look both ways, girls."

But Aggie's question lingered.

"I'm at P.S. 278. You know, the big one near Food Bazaar," said Aggie. "Are you going there, too?"

Coo knew which school that was. She'd asked Tully about it one day when they'd passed by during recess. Tons of kids played in the yard, more kids than she'd ever seen anywhere at once.

"We're still figuring that out, Aggie," Tully said. "I wasn't expecting Coo to be here this long, and enrolling in school takes a while."

Coo looked at Tully, startled. She'd never mentioned going to school like it would really happen.

"I hope you go to my school," said Aggie. "Maybe we could even be in the same class! School would be a lot better if we were together."

"I'm sure it would be," said Tully.

Coo felt Tully's grip tighten on her hand. Tully stared down the street like she was searching for something faraway. She did not look like she was sure of anything at all.

When they reached the street the alley branched off from, Coo grabbed Aggie's hand and dashed ahead.

"Wait!" Tully shouted after them, but Coo and Aggie ignored her.

Coo showed Aggie how to pull the gate open on its chain and duck in.

The alley was chilly and shadowed. Most of the snow was gone, leaving patches of slush and wet gravel, but there were still some piles in the places the sun never warmed. A soft ringing came from beyond the solid fence at the end of the alley. The trains in the rail yard were on the move, their wheels singing on the tracks. The familiar sound made Coo feel joyful.

"Flock! Flock!" Coo cried in pigeon. "Here, me! With food, me!"

The flock came streaming down from the roof into the alley.

"Wow." Aggie's mouth dropped open. "Where did you learn that?"

"From the birds," said Coo. "Throw the bread. They will come."

They ripped open the sack and began tearing the bread into tiny pieces. Pigeons crowded around, jostling one another on the gravel to reach the food.

"That's New Tiktik," Coo said, pointing. "There is Hoop, the old brownish one. That is Ka . . ."

"New human?" Ignoring the bread, Roohoo landed on Coo's shoulder and stared suspiciously at Aggie. "Face windows?"

"Face windows?" Coo laughed. "Oh. Glasses, those are. My new friend, her," she said, or tried to. *Friend* wasn't really a word in pigeon. What she really called Aggie was her new flock mate.

"Hmph," said Roohoo, and flew back up to the roof.

"He is a really grumpy pigeon," Coo said to Aggie. "His name is Roohoo."

Aggie was staring at her strangely.

"Are you *talking* to them?"

"I . . ."

"How?" Aggie's mouth dropped open. "That's amazing!"

"It's . . . secret."

"Don't run ahead, girls!" huffed Tully, finally catching up to them.

"And don't shout for the birds, please, Coo! I thought you knew better than that. Remember how we're not really allowed back here? If you can't stay calm and quiet, we'll have to leave."

Coo stared at the jumble of birds and squeezed the bread bag in her hands. She felt heat rising up her cheeks. She glanced up at Tully and was relieved to see she looked more nervous than angry.

"Tell me more of the bird names, Coo," said Aggie.

Coo pointed out Pook and Old Tiktik and several others. She was glad they had so much bread, and the seed from Tully's paper sack, too. Not only because the pigeons were clearly hungry, but also because eating kept them from trying to talk to her. She wasn't sure how she would explain her ability to Aggie, especially in front of Tully.

"It's so creepy back here." Aggie peered at the boarded-up hut and the empty factory building.

"I didn't know there was stuff like this in our neighborhood. I wonder how long ago people abandoned this place."

"It's a little bleak, isn't it?" said Tully. "But it's also peaceful. I never felt in danger here. The rail yard is right over beyond that fence," she said, pointing behind the hut. "And there are always pigeons for company."

They were down to the last slice of bread when they heard the sound of a car. There were rattles and thunks, then a big metallic *creak*.

"Someone is opening the gate." Tully's eyes went wide and she looked around the alley. "That never happens. Girls, quick. Back here." Tully pulled Coo and Aggie behind the hut.

A white van with black lettering on the side came bouncing down the alley in a crunch of gravel and parked about twenty feet up from the hut. The pigeons rose in panic and retreated to the roof.

Aggie had stooped down and was peering through an evergreen bush. "The city health department?" she whispered. "That's what the van says."

Coo crawled down beside her. The snow was ankle deep and very cold on her hands and knees, even with her mittens and heavy corduroy pants.

"The *health* department? Is that what you said, Aggie?" whispered Tully. She stood behind the hut, shaking her head. "How strange. Don't move, girls. Maybe they won't mind we're here, but I don't want to risk it. Let's just see if the van leaves quickly."

"What's the health department?" Coo asked.

Tully put a finger to her lips and shook her head. Aggie started to say something, and Tully hissed, "Shh!"

The van did not leave quickly. Two men jumped out, slamming the doors. One man was like a telephone pole, tall and thin. The other was like a fire hydrant, short and squat. They wore dark blue pants and matching jackets with round logos and lettering on the back.

The evergreen bush had a very strong pine odor. Coo felt her nose tickle. She just barely managed to hold back a sneeze, snorting into her mitten.

As Coo watched, pinching her nose, the short man barked directions to the tall one, who shuffled around the back of the van with a grim look.

"Hurry up, Frank. We're due over at the scrap yard in Willets Point in an hour for the next count. You gotta move faster."

"I'm hurrying, Stan, I'm hurrying."

"If that's hurrying I don't want to know what slow looks like." Stan's voice was hard and loud, like a honking car horn.

Frank hauled two bags out of the back of the van.

"You've looked miserable ever since we started this project," Stan continued. "What gives?"

"Don't you kind of feel bad for them?" asked Frank.

"For the *pigeons*? They're rats with wings."

Aggie shot Coo an anxious look. Coo looked back at her, confused. These men didn't seem very nice, but she wasn't sure why they would make Aggie worried, either. Coo glanced the other way. Tully was standing pressed against the hut with her eyes shut. Her hands were clasped together and it looked like she was whispering something under her breath. Coo turned back to look at the men in the alley.

"They aren't hurting anyone," said Frank. "Especially not out here in the middle of nowhere."

"The rail yard was one of the places picked *because* it's out in the middle of nowhere. People won't notice and get upset while the mayor works out the details, before it goes citywide." Stan scowled and jabbed a finger at Frank's chest. "Mayor Doherty is doing a good thing. We're lucky to help him launch this project."

"Maybe."

"*Maybe?* What's wrong with you, Frank?"

Sighing, Frank looked down at the ground.

Then he squinted. "Looks like there's already birdseed and bread here. Weird."

"What?" Stan stared down, too. "Who put it there? We're the only guys assigned to this site."

"I don't know. I don't like this place," said Frank. "It's spooky. This whole project gives me a bad feeling."

"Oh, whatever. We're wasting time!" said Stan. "Mayor Doherty's plan for the pigeons is going to make the whole city better, no ifs, buts, or maybes. Now where's your click counter? We need to quit yakking so the pigeons will come back. Hand me the bread."

Their words tumbled through Coo's head. She only understood some of what they said. The short one was mad about something, and the tall one sad. Something that involved pigeons. It didn't occur to her that it could be anything bad for the flock until she glanced at Tully and then Aggie again, and saw their faces. Both looked wide-eyed and stricken. Coo's stomach flipped like a pancake.

Stan tossed chunks of bread to the gravel. The pigeons were slowly returning to eat. Frank held a small silver ball in one hand and was making it click over and over while he stared at the feasting birds.

Suddenly the itch in Coo's nose came back. She couldn't stop it this time. She sneezed.

"What was *that*?" said Stan.

At Stan's holler, the pigeons abandoned the food for the roof.

"My count's ruined." Frank sighed.

"Someone's back here," said Stan. "No one's supposed to be back here."

A moment later Tully, Aggie, and Coo were face-to-face with a scowling Stan.

"Good morning, ladies. You're trespassing on city property. Is that birdseed? And bread?" The short man scowled at the paper sack in Tully's hand and the plastic bag with a single bread slice in it in Coo's. "Are you feeding pigeons?"

Tully had turned paler than new snow.

"Feeding pigeons is not illegal, sir," she said in a trembling voice.

"Trespassing is illegal. And you have children with you; that makes it double illegal in my book. Get going."

Tully mumbled apologies and scurried up the alley past the van, dragging Coo and Aggie behind her.

"Wait," Stan barked. "Let me see your ID."

Tully skidded to a stop. Her hand tightened around Coo's. Aggie sprinted ahead to the bend in the alley and looked back, jumping up and down in place.

"Of course," Tully said very calmly. She let go of Coo's hand, pulled out her wallet, and handed Stan a small card. "I don't drive."

Stan's eyes grew very tiny as he studied the card, then handed it back to her. His nose twitched. "How much did you and those kids hear, Ms. Bettina Tully?"

"Excuse me?" Tully froze just like pigeons sometimes did when they knew there was no way out of a hawk's talons.

"I asked, how long were you back there eavesdropping?"

Coo looked at the hut and was startled to see Roohoo perched there, observing them. None of the other pigeons had returned.

"You lost your voices or something?" said Stan.

"We love pigeons." Coo blurted out the words without thinking.

Tully sucked in her breath.

"I love pigeons, too, sweetheart." Stan's suspicious sneer morphed into a sickly sweet smile. "So does Mayor Doherty. We're here to help the city and the pigeons, too. See that bread? We're also feeding them. We're working on a plan to make things better for everyone. Cleaner."

Coo studied Stan. There was something about him she didn't like.

"Don't bother these people, Stan," said Frank.

"They're harmless. Let's keep moving. We can come back here to finish up with the real stuff later. We don't need a perfect count."

Before Stan had a chance to ask any more questions, Tully turned and pushed Coo ahead of her up the alley, toward Aggie.

"Stay off city property, Grandma!" Stan shouted after them. "Next time I'm getting the cops!"

Chapter Seventeen
No One Counts Pigeons

They went straight home. Tully sat in her blue chair and started knitting furiously, her face lined and crumpled like a piece of balled-up newspaper. Coo and Aggie sat together on the loveseat half watching cartoons but mostly glancing over at Tully. She had been nearly silent on the walk back to the apartment and had barely spoken since opening a tin of almond cookies for them.

"Those were definitely bad guys," Aggie

whispered to Coo. "And no matter what that short one said, I do *not* think they like pigeons."

"Tully?" Coo asked finally, her mouth full of cookie. Queenie sat in her lap, and Burr on her shoulder. "Who were they?"

"Don't talk while you're chewing, please, Coo," said Tully. "The men were city workers counting the flock."

"Why?" asked Coo.

"It seems they think pigeons are a problem." Tully focused on her knitting, squinting to pick up a dropped stitch. "Some people think there should be fewer."

"Fewer *pigeons*?" Coo laughed. "No way."

"It's happened before." Tully sighed. "Years ago some friends of mine fought with the city to make them stop killing pigeons. I thought that was behind us."

"Killing pigeons!" Coo was shocked. Was it possible Roohoo was right about humans?

"Some people think pigeons are pests," said Tully.

"Pests?" asked Coo. She didn't know that word.

"Bad animals," said Tully. "Things that make trouble for humans."

"Pigeons do not make trouble for humans!" Coo said. If anything, it was the other way around, she thought.

"Of course *we* don't think so, Coo," said Tully. "I love pigeons. They're intelligent, gentle, and charming. They don't bite, and they're compassionate and resourceful. And lots of people agree with us that pigeons are wonderful."

"I think pigeons are wonderful," said Aggie. "I don't think they're pests, or rats with wings. Even though my sister calls them that sometimes."

"Rats?" Coo blinked. "Pigeons? No!"

Rats were tiny-eyed, sooty creatures that rooted around the trash bins outside Tully's building. The first time she saw one, Coo screeched. They had long teeth and were ugly in a way that scared her. Tully had told her how rats stole garbage, broke into human homes, and sometimes even bit people.

 Pigeons were kind. Pigeons kept to themselves. Pigeons were beautiful.

They ate trash, true, but they were cleaner about it. They were not like rats. How could humans think that?

"Some people disagree with us about pigeons. Quite strongly, too." Tully shook her head. "Usually they don't go so far as to want to get rid of them, though."

"Tully, are they going to hurt my flock?"

"Let's hope not, sweetie."

"We have to stop them!" cried Aggie.

"You're right. I should call up some of my friends from the pigeon-rescuing world to get on their case," said Tully. "I've been out of touch for a while, though."

"We should tell the city that they need to stop hurting pigeons," said Aggie. "Maybe that would help. We can go to City Hall and tell them."

A tiny smile flickered across Tully's face, followed by a deep frown. "If only it worked like that," she said. "Mayor Doherty doesn't listen to little people like us."

"Who is Mayor Doherty?" asked Coo.

"I always forget how new you are," said Aggie. "He's the mayor!"

"Mayor?"

"He runs the city," said Tully. "He ran on a campaign about making everything 'clean,' as he always puts it. What he really means is bland, expensive, and good for very rich people."

"Lots of people hate him," said Aggie. She shifted to sit on her knees. "My grandma always said he is greedy. He only cares about getting richer. And he is obsessed with making the city look spotless!" Aggie spread her arms wide. "He got rid of a bunch of gardens people had made in empty places, because he thought they looked too messy. My dad wrote about the protesters."

"Well, he also wanted the land the gardens were on to make into new apartment buildings," said Tully.

"For rich people," said Aggie.

"They were very fancy buildings when they were finally built, that's true," said Tully. She put down her knitting, and Burr quickly shuffled off Coo and onto Tully's shoulder. "And it's true he did say the community gardens were too wild looking and unkempt. Of course Doherty wants to bother pigeons. I should have guessed."

"But what is a mayor?" asked Coo.

"Like a king," said Aggie, which didn't help much. "The king of the city!"

"Not exactly, Aggie, though goodness knows he'd like to be," said Tully. "He was elected. People voted for him, and he won." Tully paused. "Barely."

"Not my mom and dad," said Aggie. "They would never vote for him."

Tully and Aggie tried to explain to Coo about elections, and voting, and terms, and how—unlike a king—Doherty couldn't be mayor forever, not in the United States, at least.

"Tell him people *love* pigeons. Doesn't know, maybe," said Coo. "Where is he?"

"City Hall," said Aggie.

"Where's that?"

"Across the river," said Aggie. "That's where all the mayor stuff happens."

"Let's go see him! Right now," said Coo. "We will tell him we love pigeons."

"Coo," sighed Tully. "There are eight million people living in the city. We can't all just go get a meeting with the mayor."

"Eight million?" asked Coo. "How much is that?"

"Well, it's eight million," said Tully. "It's a lot."

"How much is a lot?"

Plopping her knitting down on the chair, Tully stood up and went over to the table. She reached into the sugar bowl and scattered a spoonful of crystals into her palm. "How many bits of sugar are in my hand?"

"A hundred?" guessed Aggie.

"At least! Now imagine that every grain of sugar is a person, and this whole room is full of sugar. That's how many people there are in the city. Maybe more."

Coo blinked. Even Aggie looked impressed.

"More humans than pigeons, Tully? Here?"

Both Aggie and Tully laughed. Coo's cheeks burned.

"Oh, honey. I'm sorry. Yes. There are many more people. In our city and in the whole world. There are eight million people here in this city, but seven *billion* humans on Earth." Tully dumped the sugar from her hand into the sink and started putting the clean dishes away. "A billion is much bigger than a million."

"How many pigeons, Tully?" asked Coo.

"To be honest I'm not sure," said Tully. "No one counts them, really. I mean, those guys were counting them today, but pigeons aren't usually counted, at least not for good reasons."

This wasn't how Coo imagined Earth, not at

all. Somehow she thought, in spite of everything she'd learned about the world, that there had to be more pigeons than people on the planet.

"Humans should count pigeons for good reasons," Coo said. "Now!"

"Definitely," said Aggie.

"Of course, girls. But alas, pigeons don't vote. And nothing happens unless *people* demand it."

"We should demand it, then," Aggie shouted. "People for pigeons!"

"People for pigeons!" Coo cried.

But inside, she wasn't sure. Could pigeons really trust humans? She wondered what Burr would think if he could understand what she was saying. He would think it was right. He always saw the good in humans, unlike some of the others in the flock.

"We can have a protest," said Aggie. "With signs and stuff."

"It takes a lot of work to organize some-thing like that," said Tully. "But it's a good idea, Aggie."

"Need to see the pigeons right now," Coo said. She felt sick with worry.

Tully shook her head firmly. "Absolutely not. Did you see how the man named Stan looked at my ID? I could get in huge trouble if we go back," she said.

"What if they hurt the flock tonight?" asked Coo. Suddenly anxious, she scooped up Burr and cuddled him.

"I am quite sure they won't," said Tully. She put away the last dish, then sat back down in the blue chair. "Not right now. They were just counting them. And we don't really know if they are planning anything bad; I'm just guessing. Anyway, you shouldn't worry. The city always takes forever to actually do anything, good or bad."

"They were pretty rude," Aggie said, scowling. "I don't trust them."

"Nobody is saying we should trust them," said Tully. "It's almost dinnertime, now, Aggie. Take the rest of these cookies up to your family and say good night to Coo and Milton, okay?"

Chapter Eighteen
Pigeon Roof

After Christmas came New Year's Eve, with shiny paper hats from the dollar store and little noisy things called kazoos that made Burr jump. Outside, the dark streets rang with bangs and shouts and laughter. It snowed lightly. Coo stayed up later than she ever had before but still fell asleep before the clock reached midnight and the next year began.

Tully bought a brand-new calendar at the drugstore. It was full of different birds: parrots, penguins, finches, ravens. Coo flipped through the months again and again, looking at them. These birds lived all over the world, in all kinds of wild green places. There were no pictures that looked like Coo's neighborhood and no pigeons. Coo thought about what Tully had said about people and pigeons—that no one counted them for good reasons, and not everyone thought they were wonderful. Humans celebrated so many kinds of birds, but not pigeons, it seemed. It made Coo feel angry and sad.

Aggie went back to school, and the apartment was very quiet. She had too much homework to come over in the evenings.

Coo spent a lot of time trying to knit a tiny red scarf for Queenie. Knitting was every bit as hard as it looked, and the scarf was turning out very lumpy, but Queenie didn't seem to mind.

"Please visit the flock!" Coo begged over and over, but Tully was firm.

"That man from the city saw my ID. He knows

my name. Do you understand how serious tres-passing is?" Tully sighed. "No, you probably don't. Birds don't believe in those sorts of rules."

Even Burr took Tully's side.

"Safer here, us," he told Coo. "Flock take cares of flock. Don't worry, you."

But Coo couldn't help it.

One morning a few days after Aggie started school again, on the calendar square that read Saturday, the doorbell rang. Coo was so excited she had to jump up and down while Tully peered through the peephole.

"I'm back!" Aggie shrieked when Tully finally opened the door. "Did you miss me?"

Coo had missed her so much, all her human words failed her, and she could only nod.

It was a warm day, for winter. "January thaw," Tully called it, so they decided to go to a place Coo had never been: the park.

She'd glimpsed the park a few times on walks with Tully. It was a square block of tangled-looking metal bars and planks and rubber flaps on chains, surrounded by benches and some trees. A big metal fence marched all the way around it. Coo wasn't sure she wanted to go to the park.

Aggie said the park was fun. "We can maybe use some of the swings in our dance, if it's not too busy." They were still working on *Pigeon Roof*. "But first let's just swing like normal."

The park was breezy and sun-bright when they arrived. Some tiny kids were playing on the jungle gym with their mothers, but Aggie and Coo had the things Aggie called swings all to themselves. Tully sat on a bench knitting a peach-pink sweater vest for Coo. She said she would make a matching one for Aggie, too, and a sling for Burr from the same yarn.

Coo had never been on a swing before. Aggie leaped on one and started pumping her legs, but Coo only stood next to hers, touching the seat with one mitten. It wobbled, and she took a step back.

Aggie slowed, dragging her feet against the bouncy rubber padding on the ground, until she came to a stop. She frowned.

"Don't like it? Does it make you feel queasy?"

Coo didn't know what *queasy* meant. Taking a deep breath, she plopped down on the swing, grabbed the chains in both hands, and began shuffling her feet back and forth, then kicking. Nothing happened.

"Wait." A look of astonishment passed over Aggie's face. "You don't know how. They don't have swings in—that place you're from? Here. Let me show you."

Aggie showed Coo how to lean back and kick at the same time, and within minutes all of Coo's fears dissolved into bliss. She swung up high, high, high enough to see the tops of the small baby trees that ringed the park. The sky was suddenly close. Wind whipped the bangs on her forehead under her hat. She forgot her worries about the flock. Swinging was like flying!

Finally Aggie slowed down and stopped, and so did Coo. She felt a little dizzy.

"See, it's fun," Aggie said, smiling. "I wish we could swing every day, all day. And read books. No school. Did you start at your new school yet?"

Coo's fizzy joyful feeling turned flat. "No," she said, shaking her head.

"Are you starting soon?"

"No."

"But everyone goes to school. Is Tully going to homeschool you or something?"

"Yes," Coo said, even though she didn't quite understand Aggie's question. She didn't want to talk about school anyway.

"Huh. Well, if she changes her mind, you can come to my school and be in my class." Aggie looked thoughtful. "I wonder if you get to pick your teacher when you start at a new school. Anyway, you should pick mine, Ms. Krug. She's nice. You know, she likes birds, too! We have two class parakeets, Francine and Floyd." Aggie paused and tilted her head. "Parakeets are tiny tropical birds. They're cute. They come in, like, neon colors. Like highlighter pens? Francine is yellow and Floyd is blue."

Birds. Suddenly Coo thought of the flock. What if Frank and Stan were in the alley right now, hurting them? Tully wouldn't let her check on them. Coo's eyes filled with tears that were very hot in the cold air.

"Are you crying?" Aggie's face fell. "Wait, what's wrong? Are you upset about school? Did you have a bad experience with parakeets?"

"Tully won't let me see them," Coo managed to whisper.

"See who?"

"My flock. The pigeons."

"Oh!" said Aggie. "Because Tully is scared to

go back there? Yeah, those guys were really weird and bad."

"Maybe they hurt my flock."

"I wouldn't worry. Why would the flock be hurt?" Aggie shrugged. "I was thinking about this more. They're birds. They have wings. If someone tries to hurt them, they can just fly away!"

Coo dragged her toe on the ground under the swing and studied the line her shoe made on the rubbery black surface.

"Sometimes Sugarplum goes out on the fire escape, and I worry something will happen to him," Aggie said more softly. "Like he'll go down to the street and get hit by a car, or someone will kidnap him. But he's always okay. Animals are good at taking care of themselves. Popo always told me that."

Coo began to cry harder. She didn't want to think about cats on fire escapes, even fluffy sweet ones like Sugarplum, but she also knew Aggie was just trying to be kind.

"Hey, we could ask my brother Henry or

someone to check the alley and the pigeons! Would that make you feel better?" asked Aggie. "He wouldn't be scared of those guys."

"Maybe," whispered Coo. She felt shy thinking about Aggie's brother and sister.

A small cream-and-purple pigeon was pecking its way around the swing sets, part of a flock that was scattered around the playground. Staring at her, Coo suddenly got an idea.

Coo rubbed her eyes against the sleeve of her coat and then kneeled as close as she could to the bird.

"Help me, you," she said. "Need to check on my flock, me."

The pigeon made a shocked gurgle and flapped backward.

"Mean no harm, me!" Coo cried.

Two more pigeons, bolder ones, swooped down and landed near Coo.

"Speak, you!" said the larger one, a male with speckled white-and-black feathers like cookies and cream. "How?"

"Strange!" said the other, who was all shades of purple and gray. "Humans, speak? Never!"

"Speak, me," Coo said.

In the mysterious way pigeon flocks always seemed able to communicate, all at once the others were around them, streaming from every part of the playground in a rush of wings.

"Coo?" said Aggie, wide-eyed and sitting very still on her swing as the birds zoomed around her. "Um . . . what is happening?"

"How!" an older gray bird said, landing on Coo's outstretched hand. "Explain, you!"

"Learned from my flock, me," said Coo. Nervously she looked over at the bench where Tully sat and was relieved to see she was hunched over, scowling at her knitting. Coo recognized the look. Tully had dropped another stitch. That always took a while to fix.

"Coo?" Aggie left the swing and crouched down beside her. "Are you talking to them?"

"Um. Sort of," said Coo.

"Speak more, you!" the bird on her hand demanded. "From where, you?"

"That strange flock," said the bird who was very purple. "Heard about them. Living with a human, them."

"Didn't think you were real, me," said a ragged-looking bird the color of sidewalk concrete, who was peering at Coo carefully. "Special, you. Very special."

Just like the time she helped the injured pigeon outside Goodwill so long ago, it turned out that some of the pigeons were dimly aware of her.

"Know my flock, you?" Coo asked each bird. "Fly to them, you? Speak to them, you?"

Coo tried to describe where her flock lived, and the suspicious visitors from the city, and why she couldn't visit on her own. She asked if anyone could go check on them.

But none of the pigeons knew exactly where her flock or her roof was.

"Many flocks, here," said the concrete-colored bird. "Many roofs."

"Sick flocks, heard of those," piped up a very tiny pigeon. "Many dead. Not here."

Coo's heart began to pound. She slowly stood up and began to walk back toward the swing. The pigeons flapped and scurried around her, pelting her with random questions she was too overwhelmed to answer.

"Coo, how did you learn pigeon?" asked Aggie, following her. "Wait, are you okay?"

"No," Coo murmured. She felt tears burning at her eyelids again and pressed her rough wool mittens against them. Then she took a ragged breath and looked at Aggie. "Something to tell you. Secret, okay?"

"Wow," Aggie said when Coo had finished telling her everything, from her life with the flock and Milton Burr on the roof, to how she came to live with Tully and why she wasn't in school.

They were sitting on the swings again, whispering quietly, shielded from Tully's view by a big oak. Sharing with Aggie made Coo feel relieved, like drinking a huge gulp of a puddle after a long time with no rain.

"You believe me?" Coo asked.

"Of course I do!" said Aggie, rattling her swing's chains for emphasis. "It makes everything about you make sense. The way you talk, and the wild way you can talk to birds." She shook her head. "It's totally nuts! But I believe you. You believe *me*, right?"

Coo nodded, relieved.

"Do you know how famous you'd be if you told people about your life?" Aggie peered at Coo. "I guess it would be bad, too. I don't think you'd get to be a normal kid." She bit her lip. "Also, where is Dovecotia? Are your real parents there?"

"No. Tully made it up. I lived in a dovecote. A house for pigeons. On my roof. We didn't call it a dovecote." Coo made the soft, whooshing sound of the pigeon word for *dovecote*. Aggie tried and failed to copy it.

"Pigeon is a hard language," said Aggie. "But why can't you go to school?"

"Because of rules." Coo felt another wave of relief as the human words flowed out of her mind and mouth. At least some things were getting much easier. "No one knows I live with Tully."

"And Tully's freaked out?"

"Yes. Someone could take me away. It's a secret."

"Don't worry. I won't tell anyone, I promise. I'll pinky swear."

"Pinky swear?"

"I bet you've never pinky sworn about anything, have you? Being from Dovecotia and all." Aggie giggled. "Or do pigeons pinky swear with their toes? They're so much smarter than I even thought." She looked thoughtful. "Anyway, you aren't allowed to break a pinky swear. Here."

Aggie showed her how to hook their pinky fingers together.

"I promise not to tell anyone your secrets, Coo." Aggie looked her in the eye and shook her pinky. "There! Now you don't have to worry."

Walking back from the park, something strange happened.

While they waited for a light to change on the busy road, Tully looked up at a bus stopped beside them and gasped.

"Behind me, Coo," she snapped, pushing Coo to one side.

"Why?" Coo asked.

"What's going on, Tully?" Aggie asked.

Tully didn't reply. Her whole face was a mask of worry. The light changed and she hurried them home, refusing to explain. Coo stared back at the bus as it disappeared down the boulevard.

What had Tully seen?

Chapter Nineteen
Lucia

Once they were back in Tully's kitchen, it was easy to forget about the strange incident with the bus. Tully made a pot of mint tea and opened a box of half-priced strawberry donuts from Food Bazaar.

"Mmm. These were my favorite kind of donut when I lived in Dovecotia," said Coo.

Tully looked up, confused.

Coo caught Aggie's eye, and they exchanged

tiny smiles. Coo only just managed to keep herself from laughing.

There was a knock at the door.

"Aggie, that must be Octavia," said Tully. "Will you get it? See if she wants a snack, too."

Aggie tugged open the door.

A tall, frowning woman with sharp cheekbones and frizzy red hair stood there. She wore a long purple coat and purple snow boots, and from her ears bobbed two itty-bitty avocado halves. Coo stared. Where did she get such tiny fruit? And why would anyone hang food from their earlobes? Lucia was baffling.

"You're not Octavia," said Aggie. She pushed her glasses up her nose and frowned.

"No, dear. I'm Lucia. Who are you?" Lucia's gaze flickered from Aggie to Tully to Coo. "Another niece?"

"Hello, Lucia. I thought I saw you on that bus," said Tully, her voice strange. "I'm glad you dropped by."

"I'm just relieved you're okay!" Lucia raised her eyebrows. "I keep calling and calling, and I wasn't sure anyone else would check up on you if something was wrong. What's going on? Did I do something to offend you?"

"You didn't do anything, Lucia." Tully sighed. "Aggie, you should head home now. Octavia will be back soon, and you can come over to play again tomorrow."

"We're going to visit my cousins tomorrow." Aggie pouted. "It'll take all day. And then it will be Monday."

"Well, we'll definitely miss you," Tully said. "I'm sorry."

Aggie looked at Tully, then at Coo.

"Can Coo come upstairs with me?" asked Aggie.

"No," said Tully. "Coo should stay here."

Aggie gave Coo a worried look.

Coo bit her lip. She felt anxious, too.

"Everything is fine, Aggie," said Tully. "I just need to speak with Lucia."

"No, I can go," said Lucia, stepping back through the doorway. "I really don't want to cause—"

"No, Lucia, please stay," said Tully. "Aggie, come back down if you have any problems or if Octavia is late, okay?"

Aggie gathered up her coat, hat, and mittens very slowly and walked even more slowly toward the door. She gave Coo a hug and Burr a kiss and slid out into the hall. The door closed softly behind her.

"I've been avoiding your phone calls, Lucia. I'm sorry," Tully said in the silence that followed. "It has nothing to do with anything you did."

"What's going on, then?" Lucia took off her coat and boots and hat. Her penny-colored hair frizzed up in a soft cloud. "You're not acting like the Tully I know and love."

"I'm sorry. I'll explain, or try to." Tully rubbed her temples. "Can I make you some tea? Some coffee?"

"Coffee would be nice."

Lucia and Coo sat together at the round little table while Tully brewed a pot of coffee. Coo's heart beat very fast. She cuddled Burr in her arms and tried not to look at Lucia. She could feel Lucia's eyes on her. She glanced up for a moment and saw that Lucia was smiling.

"No need to worry. I'm not as scary as I look," Lucia said. "What's your pigeon's name again?"

"Burr. Milton Burr."

"Nice outfit he's wearing there," said Lucia. "Tully's always caring for stray birds. Not my cup of tea, but I do admire her compassion. What I would love to know, though, is how did she wind up with you, Coo?"

Coo froze. So did Tully, standing beside the table with two mugs and the jug of milk.

"I *know* both you and Ben were only children.

Why won't you tell me what's really going on?" Lucia looked sad. "I know it's none of my business, but I used to think we were friends, Tully. Why have you been ignoring me?"

Coo never knew silence could be so loud.

"I've been avoiding you because—because I'm in trouble," said Tully. She slowly set the mugs and milk down on the table. "It has to do with Coo."

"I had a feeling it was all connected," said Lucia.

"I'm hoping—" Tully paused, then took a deep breath. "I'm hoping you can help me."

"Of course I want to help you, Tully. Why didn't you tell me sooner you were in trouble?"

"I've been scared."

"Scared? Why?" Lucia looked from Tully to Coo and back again. "Is someone threatening you? Where did Coo come from? Whose child is she?"

"Tully rescued me," Coo blurted out.

"Coo, wait," said Tully. "Let me—"

"Rescued you from where?" Lucia turned to Coo. "Tully's long-lost sister?"

"Coo's not really my niece," Tully said quietly.

"From my flock," said Coo. "On the roof."

"Your flock of what?" Lucia blinked, then frowned. "On what roof?"

"I can explain," said Tully. "It will take a while, though."

"I don't need to be anywhere," said Lucia. "And believe me, I want all the details."

Tully poured milk and sugar into the coffee cups and told Lucia everything: how after the post office forced her out, she started feeding the pigeons in the alley more often, and about the day she crossed paths with Coo, who gave her Milton. She explained about knowing Coo needed help and how she came back with the police, who didn't take her seriously. Tully described visiting every day, hoping to find Coo, and glimpsing her on the roof once. She told Lucia about how the police wouldn't promise to check again when the blizzard was on its way, so she went out in the storm to find Coo herself.

Lucia listened, nodding. Her eyes went wide at times, and at other times she wrinkled her eyebrows like she wasn't quite sure she believed what she was hearing. A few times she ran her hands through her hair and shook her head, like she was truly shocked.

Sometimes Coo interrupted Tully and told her own parts of the story. She told Lucia about learning to speak and live like a human. About her first trip to Food Bazaar, and about her favorite new foods and the amazing warmth of real clothes. She described her years with the pigeons and how she spoke their language. She talked about Aggie and ballet.

Outside the light grew dim. Purplish dusk arrived, and the yellow lamps on Tully's street lit up.

Lucia asked about how Coo survived, how she ate, and about Coo's real parents. Who were they? Why did they leave her in the alley? But no one could answer those questions. Not even Burr.

Lucia stood up and paced back and forth in

front of the table. "I don't know where to begin,"
she said.

"I know. And I'm so sorry I've been avoiding
you, Lucia." Tully looked at her and seemed to
wince. "I'm sorry. I've just been terrified. It made
me panic."

"I get it, and I won't hold a grudge. I'm just a bit
shocked." Lucia sighed. "You're in a very difficult
spot."

"I want to adopt Coo. I want it more than anything." Tully looked up at Lucia. "Do you know
anything about how to do it? Especially for someone in my situation?"

"Of course, when I was a caseworker I used to
handle adoptions all the time. None this like this,
though, I'll give you that."

Tully's shoulders slumped.

"But maybe it's not hopeless," said Lucia. She
sat down at the table again and patted Tully's
hand. "Let's see. There are qualifications you'd
have to meet."

"I know I would need to move," Tully said quietly. "I looked that up."

"Yes. You need at least two bedrooms."

"I don't know if my pension income is enough, or if I'm too old."

"I wouldn't worry about that as much."

"What would you worry about?"

"How Coo came to live with you. The fact that you didn't call the police when you should have." Lucia made a low whistle and shook her head. "That will be a tough one for the courts to get past. And the fact you haven't taken her to a doctor—have you?"

"I was planning on it," said Tully. "Soon . . . "

"And that we don't know where Coo really came from or if her real family is looking for—"

"The flock is my real family!" interrupted Coo. "Cared for me, them."

She could tell from the way Lucia looked at her that she didn't really believe that Coo had lived with pigeons all those years.

"Before that, you came from somewhere else," Lucia said, more gently than Coo expected. "You have a family out there somewhere. A mother who gave birth to you, though it sounds like she couldn't keep you. The state will want to try to figure out who she is."

Coo fell silent. She didn't like thinking about the things Lucia talked about. Not at all.

"I'm afraid of being rejected. Of Coo being taken away," Tully said. Her voice was strangely tight and high. "I was hoping—I was hoping we could just continue on as we are."

"But what would happen to Coo if something happened to *you*?" Lucia looked stern. "Bad things can occur at any age. Fate is unpredictable."

"I know. I've worried about that so much." Tully began to cry. Not the soft crying like when she was thinking about Ben, or the happy tears when Coo made her a card. Heavy crying. Scared crying.

It frightened Coo.

"Has Coo never seen a doctor at all?" asked

Lucia. "Not even at one of those walk-in urgent care places?"

"No," Tully whispered. "She seemed fine, and I was still figuring it out."

"The dentist?"

"Oh dear." Tully winced.

"I try to avoid thinking about the dentist, too," said Lucia. She pursed her lips. "But it's not good. Tully, I think you want to be a great caregiver for Coo, and I want to help you, but you have to take the next steps and make everything legal before anything goes wrong. Get a lawyer. Contact the police. You're my friend but if you can't do it . . . " Lucia trailed off. "You just really need to figure this out. Coo needs to get medical care, and we need to find out more about who she is."

Tully nodded. "Give me just a little time, Lucia. I'm going to straighten this out, somehow. I promise."

After Lucia left, Coo lay in her nest on the floor. She did not want to dance. She did not want to eat. She did not want to draw or talk or look at books. She stared at Tully's basket of knitting. Burr sat on her shoulder and asked her if she was sick, but she didn't know how to answer. He nudged Queenie off the loveseat and dragged her over to Coo, who gave her doll a halfhearted squeeze. Lucia had scared her so much, she could hardly think.

Tully made hot chocolate and brought two cups over—a big one for Coo and a tiny one for Queenie. "Everything will be okay," Tully said as she carefully placed the drinks on the floor. "I'm sure Lucia will help us." But she said it in a shaky, hard-swallowing way that made Coo think she was wishing and hoping, not promising.

"Lucia asks many questions!" Coo said miserably.

"She really wants to help, I think, even after how I treated her," said Tully. "I just hope I haven't done so much wrong that we can't make it right."

"She could leave us alone!"

"And how would that help us?" said Tully. "I'm honestly relieved I finally got everything off my chest. She knows the system. If anyone can help us, it's Lucia."

"We don't need help," Coo said fiercely. "We are a family, Tully."

"Of course we are. No one can change that. But we're a complicated one."

Tully pushed the hot chocolate toward her with a hopeful look. Coo dove back into her nest, pulling Queenie over her eyes. She heard Tully sigh.

The next morning was Sunday. Tully shut the door to her room and made a series of mysterious phone calls. Coo sat just outside, feeding Burr toast crumbs and trying to listen. She heard her name and the words *foster* and *adopt*, *money* and *move*, but nothing made sense.

"Scared, me," she whispered to Burr, and tried

again to explain about Lucia, authorities, and the way humans made rules about one another.

"Not scared, you," he replied. "With me, you. Safe, you."

Coo nodded, her eyes filling with tears. She hoped he was right.

Chapter Twenty
The Flock in Peril

Tully and Coo were coming back from Food Bazaar on Sunday evening, the day after Lucia's visit, when they heard a commotion in the street ahead.

It was just beginning to get dark, but in the hazy glow from the streetlamps Coo saw several people standing outside Tully's apartment building. Others were dashing back and forth on the sidewalk as if they were trying to catch something.

"I've never seen a pigeon act so crazy!" one of the observers said.

"Can pigeons have rabies?"

"Someone should call animal control. Or the cops or something."

"It's trying to break in!"

A plump purple pigeon was dashing from window to window, pecking hard on the glass, and trying to stay out of reach of the many lunging hands.

Coo recognized him instantly.

"Roohoo!"

At the sound of her voice, he sailed over and landed on her shoulder.

"Flock, sick," he panted. "Need help. Hurry!"

"What? Find me how, you?"

A man tried to grab Roohoo off Coo's shoulder. "That pigeon is seriously messed up," he said. "Girl, get it off you!"

Coo dodged him and turned to Tully. "The flock needs help! Something's wrong!"

"Let's go inside." Tully's eyes darted over the crowd nervously. Most were strangers, but a few were neighbors. Tully steered Coo and Roohoo toward the stoop.

"Wait a second, lady," said a man Coo vaguely recognized. "You can't bring a pigeon inside."

"It's a pet," snapped Tully. "Mind your own business."

Lips pursed tight, Tully shoved Coo through the building's doorway and then into the apartment.

"Whew," she said, leaning against the apartment door when it was shut and locked. "Coo, what is going on? Who is this pigeon? What is it doing here?"

Coo was trying to find out, but Roohoo was so rattled he was struggling to speak. It was the first time Coo had ever seen Roohoo scared. Burr hopped over from his perch to listen.

"Strange humans came, scattered seed," Roohoo panted. "Didn't trust it, me. Flock ate it. Sick now, them. Can't fly. Okay, me. Followed you back from roof earlier, me. Remembered way again, me. Need help. Fast!"

Trembling, Coo turned to Tully.

"We have to go to the roof right now," she said. "My flock is sick!"

The first thing Coo noticed was that the chain was off the gate to the alley. Tully pushed and it swung wide open. They rushed through.

Everything else appeared normal at first: gray gravel, brown weeds, faded litter. The snow had vanished. They could hear the distant chug of the trains and a honk or two from cars on the busy streets nearby. Roohoo circled around Coo and Tully, urging them to go faster.

When she reached the hut, scampering ahead of Tully, Coo had trouble understanding what she was seeing in the dim evening light.

Pigeons were all over the ground. Huddled in groups and sprawled on their sides. Barely moving.

Coo skidded to a halt. She swallowed, and

turned, looking wildly around. New Tiktik—Ka—Hoop. Where were they? The closest pigeon was Hem. He leaned against the weedy chain-link fence, trembling.

Coo knelt, her own hands shaking, and scooped him into her lap.

"Sick, you?"

Hem blinked—his eyes were cloudy, distant—and took a ragged breath. He was about to speak when Tully arrived.

"This is horrible!" Tully wrung her hands and paced from bird to bird. She pulled out her phone.

"I'm calling Nicolas," she muttered to herself. "Oh, goodness help us."

Heart pounding, Coo turned to Hem.

"Seed," gasped Hem. "Bad . . . new . . . seed. From . . . new humans."

Scattered all around in the gravel were tiny golden kernels, different from anything Coo had seen before.

Coo reached to pick one up, but before she

could, Roohoo landed hard on her hand.

"Don't, you," he growled. "Poison."

Coo quickly drew back her hand.

"Suspicious humans," he grumbled. "Told others, me. Don't eat seed, you. Listen? No! Never listen to me, them. Now sick, them." He swept a shaky wing toward the alley, which was littered with staggering birds.

"Nicolas!" Tully shouted into her flip phone. "It's Bettina Tully. Listen, there's an emergency. The flock I feed up here has been poisoned. They're hanging on but just barely. Can you help me?"

Nicolas was a veterinarian, Tully explained in a shaky voice, while she and Coo cradled sick pigeons and moved them closer together to stay warm. He'd gone to veterinary school in the country he was born in, but here in the city he drove a taxi. He still cared for animals when he could, particularly birds, which he loved, and especially pigeons, which he loved most of all. Tully had taken sick birds to him in the past. He said on the phone he would come straight away.

"I wish Aggie was here," Coo murmured as they waited.

"Friends make life's hard moments easier, don't they?" said Tully.

Coo nodded. She was glad Burr was at home, though. She didn't want him to see what was happening to their flock.

Tully's phone buzzed. "It's Nicolas!" said Tully, picking it up. "Hello? You're almost here! Turn left at Northern Boulevard, then right . . ."

At last a yellow car came inching down the alley, headlights illuminating the pigeons on the ground. Nicolas hopped out, swinging a flashlight and a duffel bag, and began barking directions to Coo and Tully.

Coo froze. Everywhere she turned, a bird she knew and loved was lying still on the gravel and barely breathing. Hoop. Ka. Old Tiktik. How could she choose who to help first?

"Coo." A faint voice floated up from her feet. "Help me, you."

New Tiktik. Coo scooped New Tiktik into her hands and nuzzled her fresh, rain-clean feathers. The little bird was breathing fast and shallow.

"Missed you, us," New Tiktik gasped. "Need you, us. Can't fly, me."

Tears burned Coo's eyelids, but there was no time to cry. Nicolas was shouting about boxes and medicine. Tully was dashing around the alley, carefully shuffling sick pigeons into her hands.

Gingerly, Coo hugged New Tiktik to her chest and brought her to Nicolas.

"Help my friend, please."

Nicolas looked up from the pile of small cages, bags of liquids, and blankets strewn across the hood of the cab. He was a tall man with a rumpled mop of black hair and friendly, worried eyes.

"Put it in here, angel," he said, motioning to an empty plastic cage.

A wild look of fear flashed in New Tiktik's eyes as Coo bundled her into the cage. Of course she was scared. Since hatching from her egg, she had never once been confined.

"Safe, you," Coo said. "Promise you, me."

"Scared, me," New Tiktik whimpered.

"Heals you, this human. Like Tully."

Coo looked up to find Nicolas staring at her curiously. But before he could say anything, Tully arrived with Hoop and Ka, who were both very sick, too.

Soon nearly all the pigeons were in Nicolas's taxi, ready to go. Tully and Nicolas stood by the car's hood, fussing over Pook, who was particularly weak. Scrambling between the boxes, Coo counted the birds, and then counted again. At least it was winter, and a particularly hungry one at that, so Coo guessed there were no pigeons sitting on eggs in the dovecote, and no new squabs. Only one bird was missing.

Roohoo!

He wasn't sick, but he couldn't stay in the alley or on the roof by himself. Pigeons never stayed anywhere alone. It was too dangerous. Hawks . . . cats . . . Coo shuddered.

"Roohoo?" she called out in the dark. "Come here, you!"

But no one replied.

Tully and Nicolas were disagreeing about something to do with Pook's treatment. Coo hesitated, then slipped through the old rip in the fence and began shimmying up the fire escape. Just before hoisting herself over the ledge onto the roof, she turned to look at the rail yard. Beyond it was the skyline of crooked, twinkling rectangles she'd always watched at night. Now she knew those tall buildings had many people inside them.

The roof was full of familiar shadows. Never

before had they seemed so menacing. The place seemed dingier and grayer than she remembered, too. Looking around in the dim light, Coo paused to wonder how she'd spent so many years in such a wild and rough place. Now that she was here, she didn't miss it at all. She hurried to the dovecote.

"Hello?" It was too dark to see much, but as her eyes adjusted, one lone pigeon came into view. "Roohoo?"

"Hrmph."

"Here, you? Alone? Why?"

"Not human, me."

"Take care of you, me. Come."

"Staying here, me."

"Alone! Not alone, pigeons. Ever. Roohoo, no. Come with me, you."

"Humans, all bad. Always knew it."

"Me? Tully? Bad?"

Roohoo preened his feathers instead of replying. Coo reached out to grab him, but he scurried one way, then another, and she gave up.

"Fine, you. Stay here."

Coo heard Tully down in the alley, calling her name over and over.

She turned around and left Roohoo in the dovecote.

Coo had begged to go with the pigeons in Nicolas's taxi to wherever he was taking them, but Tully and Nicolas both said no. There was no room in the car, and it was very late.

Standing by the taxi, its heat blasting to keep the sick birds warm, Nicolas put his hands on Coo's shoulders and looked her in the eye. "I promise to do everything I possibly can to help the birds," he said. "We'll know in the morning if that is enough."

That night, back at the apartment, neither Coo nor Tully could sleep. Coo read picture books from the library but stopped when she realized she was staring at the same sentences over and over. She and Tully tried to bake cookies, but they forgot to add baking powder and the cookies came out of the oven flat and hard as the sidewalk. Even Burr wouldn't eat one. Coo propped Queenie up at the kitchen table and pretended to feed them to her.

Finally Coo and Tully sat in silence with a pot of strong mint tea. It was almost midnight. Coo had never stayed up so late before, not even on New Year's Eve, but she couldn't sleep.

"I wish Aggie were here," Coo said for the hundredth time.

"Her parents would find it very strange if we rang the bell at this hour," said Tully. "It's also a school night."

Horrible thoughts bounced around in Coo's mind, troubling her.

"Tully, why do things . . . die?"

Her question hung in the air and thickened the silence.

"That's something people have been trying to answer for as long as there have been people, Coo."

"Where do pigeons go when they die?" Coo asked. "I mean, their spirits." Over the past few months, Tully had told her a little bit here and there about spirits, gods, and the universe.

"Some people think souls are always returning to the earth in new bodies, over and over again. Other people think there's a lovely place called Heaven you can go, which lasts for all eternity. And another place called hell, that's bad. Some people think nothing happens. That we are only bodies, which decay."

"What about people?" She thought of Aggie's grandmother. "Where do they go?"

"The same place as pigeons, I would think, wherever that is."

"What about Ben? Where is he?"

Tully flinched, and so did Coo.

"No, Coo. It's okay to ask these things." Tully looked down into her teacup. "I wish I knew where Ben was. Wherever he is, I would love to meet him again someday."

"How did he die, Tully?"

"He was riding a bicycle and a car hit him."

Coo was stricken. Cars killed people, just like they killed pigeons.

"I hate cars," Coo blurted out.

"Me, too, Coo," Tully said quietly. "Me, too."

"I hate that people poison pigeons. Why, Tully? Make them stop, us! How?"

"Maybe you'll be the one to figure that out someday, Coo."

"Someday is when?"

"Not today," Tully said, sighing. "Or at least not tonight. But hopefully soon."

Coo fell silent. She had to save her flock and all the other pigeons at risk—but how?

Chapter Twenty-One
The Pigeon Hospital

Slumped over the table and their cold cups of tea, Coo and Tully woke on Monday morning to Tully's phone buzzing on the table. Burr hopped on top of it, pecking the plastic case.

Tully sat up with a start. "Is it Lucia? Or the lawyer? What day is it? Oh, it's Nicolas. Hello?"

Coo rubbed her eyes. Recently she had become used to seeing worry and sadness on Tully's face. But now there was something else.

"Really? Oh my goodness, Nicolas. This wasn't the news I was expecting. How can I thank you? We'll be there in an hour or two. I remember the way. See you soon."

Tully hung up and grinned. "The flock is okay, Coo!"

Coo blinked. It was hard to believe what Tully said. But seconds later she felt a flutter of excitement mixed with relief.

"Get your shoes on. Give Burr a good-bye hug—it's too long of a trip to bring him," said Tully. "We're going on the train!"

Sharp little snowflakes were falling. Tully called them flurries. The word sounded so funny that Coo laughed, even though she was again sick with worry for her flock. What if Tully had misunderstood Nicolas? What if the flock was still in danger?

Coo and Tully joined the jumble of umbrellas heading for Steinway Street. Nicolas lived all the way at the other end of the city, Tully said. They had to take a subway to get there. It would be Coo's first time.

"Here we are," said Tully. "Our train's down there."

Coo peered into the black, damp mouth of the stairwell. People pushed past them. The stairwell belched menacing rumbles, metallic shrieks, and crackly static voices. The sidewalk trembled every few seconds.

"I don't like this," Coo murmured.

"This is how millions of people get around." Tully nudged her toward the steps, but Coo tightened her grip on the top of the railing. "It's amazing we haven't had to ride it yet. Come on."

"No, Tully."

"Come on, Coo," said Tully. "One step at a time."

With Tully coaxing her and holding one elbow, Coo took the stairs gingerly. Some people squeezed around them, muttering. Behind them, a stout woman stomped her large umbrella against the step and grumbled, "Really? Hurry up." Tully swiveled around and silenced her with a fierce stare.

Coo made it to the last soaked step, only to find the station itself was even more intimidating. Tully prodded Coo down the dark, drippy corridor toward an ever-growing roar and stopped in front of a row of silver gates. People rushed past, swiping small yellow cards through boxes and pushing their bodies against the gates so they moved. Tully took her own card out of her pocket and nudged Coo forward. It took less force than Coo expected to walk through the turning bars. Tully followed behind her and led Coo down another set of stairs, beneath which was something Coo, for all her years living above a rail yard, had never seen up close.

Her jaw dropped.

The train came clattering, growling, singing into the station just as they reached the bottom step. Like a car, but a thousand times more terrible. Coo jumped back, screaming, but the roar drowned out her voice. "Hush," Tully said. "It won't hurt you."

The train slowed. It was huge. Faces peered out its windows. Coo watched its doors open and the crowds on the platforms cram in.

The trains—humans were inside them! In all her years on the roof, she never thought about what was *inside* the trains.

"Hurry, love, it's our train."

Coo followed Tully into the crush of damp coats and dribbling umbrellas. The train lurched, and Coo grabbed a pole. Her head spun.

A few stops later, when humans poured off the train, a nice gentleman offered Tully a seat. Coo forgot her fear. Now she was just curious. She studied every face and peered out the windows when she could, even though all they showed between the places called stations was a dense blackness. Staring into the darkness, she was suddenly overwhelmed by questions. Was the flock really going to be okay? What was going to happen with Lucia?

At last they arrived at 95th Street, their station. It was just as loud and damp as the one where they'd started. They emerged onto a bright, noisy sidewalk. It was hard to understand how far they were from home. It looked almost exactly like the neighborhood they'd left, though the flurries had stopped.

They started walking, and soon the streets looked very different. Instead of just brick buildings packed tightly together, there were also houses painted different colors and small yards that were brown and gray. There was still some old blizzard snow piled up in the deepest, shadiest yards. It was very quiet.

"It's been a couple of years since I brought a sick pigeon to Nicolas," said Tully as they walked. "But everything looks the same."

They stopped in front of a tall yellow and white

house with many windows and a big porch. There was a small white gate in front, which Tully opened and shut behind them. They walked past a row of heavy evergreen shrubs and up to the front door. Coo was startled to see a bear peeking through some bushes, and behind it, a tiny bearded man in a pointed hat. She squinted. They were definitely made of stone.

"I think it's this bell," said Tully, pushing one of the three buttons.

When the door opened, all of Coo's worries seemed to explode.

"My flock!" She clutched Nicolas's arm. "Show me!"

"Coo—it's not polite to grab people—"

"No, no, I understand." Nicolas smiled at Coo. "You must be very worried. Come, let's go straight to the pigeons."

Nicolas's hair looked even wilder than it had last night. He ushered them down a hallway, past a tidy little kitchen, and then into a small room just a bit larger than a closet. "My pigeon hospital," he said. "See, I love pigeons just like Tully does."

Murmuring, hooting, cooing cages crowded the tables and shelves from floor to ceiling. Hoop, Old Tiktik, New Tiktik. Coo didn't know who to turn to first.

"Coo, here!" New Tiktik was the first to notice her. "Saved us, Coo did!"

"Here, me!" Coo whispered. She sensed it would be better not to talk too much in pigeon in front of Nicolas, but she couldn't help it.

"Feeling sick, me," said Hoop. "But worst is over."

"Thank you, Coo," Ka said gravely. "Without you, dead us."

"Really Roohoo," Coo said. "Found me, him. Saved you all, him."

"We can't thank you enough, Nicolas!" said Tully. Her voice drowned out Coo's pigeon whispers. "We almost lost them."

"We got lucky." Nicolas gently stroked New

Tiktik's feathers, smiling down at her while he spoke. "They hadn't eaten very much of the poison, and I had enough antidote on hand. But Tully, this isn't the first incident I've heard about." He paused, and his gaze roamed over the rest of Coo's flock. He shook his head and turned to Tully. "Do you remember Maureen Beasley? Picks up sick birds sometimes."

"Sure. I haven't seen her in years."

"Maureen noticed a little post on some community message board about dead pigeons under a highway overpass. She went to the spot herself. It was bad. Brought me some of the poor babies to check." Nicolas's face crumpled like an empty bag. "It was too late for them. They'd been poisoned."

"Oh no!"

"She tried to get the newspapers and even the local TV news interested, but nobody reported on it."

"That's terrible, Nicolas."

"It's the worst I've seen in years." Nicolas's eyes

filled with tears. "Who would want to hurt birds? I don't understand these people."

With Tully's help, Coo lifted Hoop out of her cage and gave her a hug. There was so much she wanted to say in both languages.

Pigeons were dying. Because of people. And it didn't sound like Tully or Nicolas or anyone else knew how to stop it.

Why did pigeons live with humans at all?

Coo fought back the urge to cry.

"I will never understand. Never." Nicolas shrugged and sighed. "At least this flock made it."

"Are they really okay, Nicolas?" Tully asked in a hushed tone.

"Yes," he said. "They need to regain their strength, but I think they will be fine."

"Well, thank you. We should let them rest, and let Nicolas get on with his day," said Tully. "Come on, Coo."

"No, no, no. You came all this way; please stay longer." Nicolas lifted his hands and looked from

Tully to Coo and back again, smiling. "Coffee? Tea? We can sit in the kitchen for a bit. Some juice for you, Coo? I have some orange juice, and some cookies?"

"No, thanks," Coo said quietly. "Stay with pigeons."

"That's fine," said Nicolas. "I'll bring you some."

Nicolas came back carrying a tall glass of orange juice and a plate piled high with small square cookies, and carefully placed them on one of the only empty surfaces in the tiny room. "All yours," he said. "Enjoy!"

"Nicolas and I will catch up in the kitchen, okay, Coo?" said Tully. "Let the birds sleep, if they need to."

As soon as Tully and Nicolas left, Coo began peppering the flock with questions. Could they still fly? Were they weak? Was Nicolas kind to them? In between questions she bit into a cookie. It had a pleasantly buttery lemon flavor. She broke

up the other cookies and fed them to
the flock, who gobbled up the crumbs.
Coo chugged down her juice.

"Very kind, him," Hoop said when
she'd finished pecking up her pieces of cookie.

"Sings to us, him," said New Tiktik. "Pretty
songs. Like a sparrow, him."

Coo smiled.

"Sick, other flocks?" asked Old Tiktik. "Hurt?"

Coo's smile vanished. She needed to tell the
pigeons what was going on, but how? She was
afraid of making them upset when they were
already so weak.

"Yes," she said finally. "More flocks sick."

"Dead?" asked Hoop. "Poisoned, them?"

Coo looked down at the floor.

"Poisoned, them," said Ka. "Dead, them."

The flock fell silent.

"Stop the poisoners, me," Coo said, raising her
head and looking at the pigeons. They stared back.
"Find a way, me. Somehow. Promise."

When Tully came back a few minutes later and told her it was really time to go, Coo didn't want to leave. She stroked each of her flock members and kissed their heads.

"Back soon, me," she whispered. "Heal fast, you."

Finally Tully took her by the arm and gently led her into the hallway, where Nicolas stood. Coo handed him her empty plate and glass.

"Thank you," Coo said. "For everything."

"Anytime!" Nicolas smiled. "You and Tully are welcome here always."

As they walked to the door, Coo noticed how many pictures Nicolas had on his walls—almost as many as Aggie's family. But Nicolas's were all of the same two people: a warm-eyed woman with puffy brown hair and a solemn little girl with dark, heavy bangs.

"Who are they?" Coo asked, pointing.

"My wife and daughter." Nicolas smiled in a

way that reminded Coo of the way Aggie smiled sometimes—like he was happy and sad at once. "My daughter's name is Victoria. She's just a little bit older than you."

"Where is she?" Coo looked down the hallway toward the kitchen and back again. Behind the pigeon hospital was a narrow room with a single bed, and beside that a tiny bathroom. There were no other rooms. The apartment was very small, and it didn't look like anyone else but Nicolas and the sick birds lived there.

"They are far away in Brazil," said Nicolas.

Coo figured that was a country. She had a vague understanding of geography from Tully, who had shown her maps and tried to teach her about the world.

"They don't live here with you?" Coo frowned. "Why?"

"Coo—"

"No, it's okay, Tully. It's good for children to be curious," said Nicolas. "They are not allowed to because they don't have the right papers yet. I'm waiting to be able to bring them here. I hope very soon."

"They need paper to come live with you?"

"Yes. A special paper called a visa that the government gives you so you can come here. Until then, they have to stay in Brazil."

"Draw your own papers?" said Coo. "I draw. I can draw them?"

"Wouldn't it be great if that was allowed?" Nicolas laughed. "No, only people in the government can give them to us. I hope they will soon. But for now we wait."

On the walk back to the train, Coo was very quiet. She held Tully's hand, lost in thought.

Coo thought about the flock. They didn't have things like papers to say where they could go. New pigeons from other places joined the flock sometimes, and no one stopped them.

She thought about the way Tully needed other

special paper—money—to buy things to eat at Food Bazaar, while pigeons just took whatever they found as theirs.

She thought about the crosswalk signs she and Tully had to watch carefully before crossing the street. It was so different from how birds just flew from place to place, not needing permission from anyone or anything.

She thought about the rules Tully had described for how humans were supposed to live—rules people like the police officers enforced. She thought about school, where Aggie had to go. Pigeons had nothing like school. They lived, and learned through life.

She thought about the decisions the people in the city government had made about pigeons. The decision to poison them. What gave them that right?

Coo felt a flush of anger. She squeezed Tully's hand so hard, Tully peered down at her.

"Are you okay?" Tully asked, frowning. "You

look so upset. You know your flock will get better, right?"

Humans were very different than birds. Maybe Roohoo had a point.

"Don't worry," said Tully. "Everything will be okay."

Coo nodded, but she wasn't sure Tully was right.

Chapter Twenty-Two
Roohoo

Tully kept her eyes shut nearly the whole subway ride home. Her face was pinched and still, like she was in pain.

Coo closed her eyes and worried, too. What would happen when the flock was well enough to return to the roof? How could she keep them safe? Her stomach lurched when she thought about it. She wondered if all of them could come live at Tully's apartment, but couldn't picture Tully being okay with that, even though she loved birds. Besides, it wouldn't help all the other pigeons in the city. She was relieved she didn't have to worry about her own flock for a few more days. Except—

Coo's eyes flew open.

Roohoo!

He had wanted to be left alone, but pigeons *never* stayed alone. It was too dangerous. He was muddled from shock.

"Tully." Coo shook her sleeve. "We have to go get Roohoo. Right away!"

The train reached a curve in the tunnel and its brakes screeched like a cat, nearly drowning out Coo's voice.

"Roohoo?" shouted Tully, wincing at the noise.

"Yes! Roohoo is on the roof alone!"

"He'll be okay, sweetie!" Tully reached over to help Coo cover her ears.

The train pulled into a dim, empty station and Coo put her hands down. The conductor announced the stop's name over a hissing intercom.

"He didn't eat any poison and knew enough not to," said Tully.

Coo shook her head. She had to make Tully understand. Humans spent time alone, but not pigeons. A pigeon without a flock was a hawk's dinner.

"Please, Tully."

"It's a very bad idea to go back to the alley right now. We don't know who might be there. What if the police caught us?"

"He will die if we don't, Tully. What if he dies!"

"All right, all right. In for a penny, in for a pound," Tully sighed. "Let's get him this evening—but quickly! No lingering."

The sun was setting pink as fruit punch as Coo ran across the roof. She had taken the spooky inside stairs two at a time and beat Tully to the top by several flights. She had been calling Roohoo's name since they reached the alley, but there was no answer. She hoped he was just ignoring her. He was such a stubborn bird.

She thought about all the times Roohoo had been mean to her over the years. She thought about all the harsh things he'd said about humans. She wondered why she was bothering to help him now. But she also agreed with him. Humans poisoned pigeons. Humans made laws that kept families far away from one another. Humans had odd, complicated things like money and dangerous, stupid inventions like cars. Roohoo wasn't wrong about them.

Besides, Roohoo was one of her flock mates. Maybe pigeons didn't feel much loyalty for individuals in their flock, but Coo was human. She couldn't bear to think of him being alone. She had to give him one more chance.

The dovecote seemed empty and forlorn. Without the sounds of the flock muttering and moving about inside, it looked more ragged and tilting than ever before.

Coo took a deep breath. Then she plunged her head inside. It was cold and smelled different—dustier.

"Roohoo?"

At the very top of the dovecote, a dim ball of feathers shifted

"Hungry, me," Roohoo said in a very small voice.

Coo sighed with relief.

"Come with me, you. Safe at Tully's house, you. Lots of food there."

Roohoo allowed himself to be scooped off the nest shelf, but he wouldn't stoop to riding on Coo's shoulder. She carried him to the stairs, and he peered into the black hole of the open doorway. Tully was just reaching the top, huffing and puffing.

"Meet you in the alley, me," Roohoo said, and zoomed away.

Tully poked her head out and stared after him, bewildered.

"Is that Roohoo?" Tully panted. "He's leaving? All these stairs for nothing?"

"We will meet him in the alley," said Coo.

"Good grief!" Tully groaned, and turned around.

Coo hurried ahead of her, worried Roohoo would change his mind. But when she got outside, he was sitting atop the boarded-up hut, staring toward the trains.

"Ready?" said Coo. "Wait for Tully, us."

Tully finally lumbered out of the broken side door of the factory, sighing, and ducked through the rip in the fence. Night had fallen.

Roohoo bobbed slightly ahead of Coo and Tully, jumping from tree branch to fence post to mailbox, sailing across the busy streets, the whole walk back to the apartment.

The next morning Coo sat at the table, drawing shapes in the leftover pools of maple syrup on her plate and half watching the TV. A dark-haired woman was singing about the number three with some kids and puppets.

Tully encouraged her to sing along. She insisted

Coo needed to practice speaking English as much as possible, even though the noise often made Coo feel like her head was hurting. Humans were so loud. She missed the quiet of pigeons.

"You can't practice too much, Coo. Eventually you'll need to go to school, and I worry about how you will cope," said Tully. "Though you are getting better and better at speaking every day."

Aggie was at school. Coo was alarmed by how many days a week school happened. She wondered if school was like TV—lots of singing and dancing.

Thump.

Coo jumped. After spending the entire night hunched in the shadows atop the fridge, ignoring Coo's bagel lure and rebuffing Burr's attempts at talking, Roohoo suddenly landed at her elbow.

"Pancake?" Coo offered, pushing some scraps his way.

Roohoo wasn't interested in pancake. He stared at the television set.

"Humans?" he whispered. "Tiny humans? Furry humans?"

Before Coo could explain, Roohoo fluttered over to the set. He pecked hard at the glass and then hopped into the dark cavern of dust bunnies behind the television.

"TV, it is." There wasn't really a pigeon word for it, but Coo tried. "Not real humans. Electricity? Zip! Zizz! Zap!" She waved her arms around, trying to remember the first time *she* had seen TV. Roohoo popped his head out from behind the set, strands of dust hanging from his feathers and beak, and stared at her suspiciously.

"Humans," he muttered finally. "Strange."

Coo trailed Roohoo as he explored Tully's apartment. It was fun, she found, to be a teacher, even if Roohoo was a difficult student.

He scrutinized her careful demonstration of the kitchen sink's faucet. "Rain, much better."

"What? Why?"

"Falls more places. Tiny bit of rain, just in here, what's the use?"

Coo moved on to the cabinets, showing him boxes of crackers and bags of birdseed. These he was much more interested in. He rolled a stray cookie crumb from the back of the shelf with his toe and carefully pecked it.

"Not bad."

Next Coo opened the freezer. Roohoo jumped in and immediately whirled back out.

"Winter!" he shrieked, beating his wings. "Horrible!"

"No, no!" Coo tried to explain it was for storing food, but Roohoo would have none of it.

"Winter in a box! Humans, so silly." He retreated to the other end of the room, behind the dusty TV again. "And dangerous."

"Dangerous?" Burr, perched on top of his cage, stopped preening his feathers and looked in Roohoo's direction. "Silly bird, you!"

Roohoo popped his head out from behind the

TV and the two glowered at each other.

Coo sighed.

On Wednesday morning the sky was so heavy and gray that Tully turned on all the lights in the apartment during breakfast. "Winter after Christmas and New Year's is bleak sometimes," said Tully. "Well, it'll be spring soon enough."

Tully was putting yesterday's dishes away and Coo was just starting her bowl of cinnamon-raisin oatmeal—sharing the raisins with Burr—when Tully's phone rang.

Roohoo zoomed from his hiding place behind the cereal boxes on the top of the fridge and plunked down next to it.

"Beetle?" he said. "Cricket?" He pecked at the phone. "Alive?"

"Quick, before he breaks it!" shouted Tully, hurrying over. "I doubt pigeon damage is under warranty."

Coo swooped the phone away from Roohoo's beak and handed it to Tully.

"It's Nicolas!" said Tully, looking at it and then opening it. "Hi, Nicolas. Is everything okay? What's the latest?" She went into the bedroom, shutting the door.

"Strange bug," Roohoo said, staring after her. "Huge bug."

"Bug? No!" said Burr, hopping from the rim of Coo's bowl to her shoulder and staring down at him. "Human talking thing, that. Not bug."

"Hrmph," said Roohoo. He didn't sound convinced.

The door opened. Tully looked grim.

"What's wrong?" Coo stood up. "What did Nicolas say?"

"I don't want to upset you," Tully murmured.

"Tell me," Coo said. She swallowed hard. What if her flock had gotten sicker? Maybe someone had taken a turn for the worse. She thought of Old Tiktik, and Hoop. They were elderly.

"Your pigeons are all okay," said Tully. "But Nicolas has asked around and checked online, and he found out about three dead flocks near his neighborhood. Whatever is going on, it's getting worse."

Coo sat back down at the table, at a loss for words. Her appetite was gone. She carefully picked out every remaining raisin in her bowl for Burr. Tully started doing the breakfast dishes, her phone tucked safely in her pocket. Roohoo sat in the middle of the table, eyeing Tully.

"Upset, you?" Burr asked Coo as he gobbled up the last few raisins.

"More pigeons hurt," Coo said, choking back tears. "Other flocks. Tully heard."

Roohoo turned around to look at her. "Tell more, you," he said. "Flocks, how many?"

Coo told him everything Tully had said.

"Leave, pigeons," Roohoo said when she was finished. "Leave humans. Fly away. Far!"

"Where?" asked Coo.

Tully came over and collected her half-filled, raisin-less oatmeal bowl. "Not hungry, Coo?"

Coo shook her head.

"Place with no humans," said Roohoo when Tully returned to the sink. "Go there, pigeons. Safe there!"

There were places like that on Earth, Coo knew. Forests, deserts, icy lands.

"Need humans, pigeons," said Burr. "Need bagels, donuts, birdseed. Need ledges, dovecotes, roofs."

"Why, pigeons?" said Coo, shocked to find herself siding with Roohoo. "Don't need humans, other birds." She was thinking of parrots, penguins, and even—with a shudder—hawks.

"Always together, pigeons and humans," Burr said. "Good and bad, bad and good. Always so."

"Change now," Roohoo grumbled. "No more humans. Pigeons leave."

Coo despaired. Roohoo was right. If humans kept trying to get rid of pigeons, why did pigeons keep living near them? She thought about the globe in the library and the videos of the vast, wild places that she'd seen on TV. There was so much empty land on Earth—more than her mind could ever hold. Why didn't pigeons go far away from humans who wanted to hurt them?

"What's the place with the least humans, Tully?" she asked.

"Antarctica, I guess," Tully said. She finished washing the last breakfast dish and turned off the faucet. "It's really cold there."

"Pigeons could go live in Antarctica," said Coo. "No people, no poison."

"And everything is ice and snow! It's much too cold for pigeons there," said Tully. She handed Coo the sponge. "Can you wipe down the table for me?"

"Penguins live there," Coo said, nudging Roohoo out of the way as she cleaned. She remembered seeing a program about it.

"They're very different from pigeons, Coo. They have different kinds of feathers, they can swim, they eat fish. And they love winter," said

Tully. "It's nearly always wintry in Antarctica."

What's dealing with a little more winter if you aren't getting poisoned? Coo didn't think the penguins would give pigeons any problems about sharing the ice and snow.

"There's no food for pigeons in Antarctica," Tully said gently. "Honey, it's all ice and ocean there. Have you ever seen a pigeon catch a fish?"

Coo stopped wiping and went over to the sink. She carefully rinsed the sponge.

"The north?" Coo said. At the library one afternoon, she had studied a picture book about her home state. North of the city there was a huge forest full of mountains and lakes. "Many trees there. Pigeons can eat . . . berries and stuff."

"That sounds nice. It's true that it gets pretty wild north of here. Lots of forests." Tully's tone was vague, as if she wasn't really thinking about pigeons or forests at all. She'd sunk into a chair at the table and was staring off at no place in particular. Coo knew that look. It was her thinking-about-problems look, and Coo didn't like it one bit.

"I will tell the flock to fly to the woods," said Coo. "So they are safe. And no more worries about anything."

A plan was hatching in her mind. When the flock was well enough to get out of the pigeon hospital, she would convince them to go north to the woods. She and Tully, and maybe even Aggie, could go with them. The pigeons had carried her to the roof once when she was a baby. Why not now, even though she was bigger? They could hook their beaks into her shirt and pants. Coo was shocked she hadn't thought of it before. Tully was a bit heavier, but the stronger pigeons, like New Tiktik, could help take her. Coo was sure of it. The authorities would never find them, nor would the pigeon poisoners.

Suddenly it all seemed so clear. Burr could ride along safely tucked into her coat. She looked at Roohoo, who was attempting to rotate the arm of Tully's pepper grinder with his beak and sprinkling black flakes all over the freshly cleaned table in the process. Pigeons were definitely clever. They would know how to make her idea work.

"Tell other flocks, too," Coo continued out loud. "Lots of pigeons could fly north to woods all together. All the pigeons! All safe."

"Sounds like a good idea," Tully said absently.

She started to share her plan with Roohoo and Burr.

"Fly north, us! Woods. Safe. No humans. Carry me, you. In beaks—"

"Carry you, us?" Roohoo scoffed. "Leave the city, you? With us, you? No. Pigeons only, no humans."

"Heavy, you," Burr added. "Big now, you. Dangerous."

Coo sighed. She didn't even bother mentioning also bringing Tully.

The week passed slowly. Aggie was too busy to visit. Coo's flock was still too sick to come home.

Something called a polar vortex arrived. The radiators hissed and clattered all day and night. The windowpanes were so cold it stung to touch them, and Tully moved her spindly little houseplant away from them to the kitchen table. It was too cold to go outside.

Instead, Coo leafed through books, drew pictures, and watched TV, as much as she could stand.

And she kept an eye on Roohoo.

Roohoo was a careful observer of how things worked. Soon he was stealing the remote and rapidly changing channels, especially when Tully tried to watch the news, which he found dull. On the third night he was in the apartment, Tully and Coo hid the remote, but within ten minutes Roohoo had learned how to press the buttons on the set itself.

"Better, this way," he insisted as the channels flashed by. He only stopped for cooking shows.

"I can't wait for the flock to get well and this bird to get out of my house," Tully grumbled. She was still annoyed by the little nicks Roohoo's beak had left on the outside of her phone.

"Having fun, me," Roohoo said to Coo the next morning as she sat on the floor by the closet trying to put the vacuum cleaner back together. He had managed to detach two of the brushes and pull the bag partway out. "Might stay here, me."

"Tully, Roohoo says he doesn't want to go back to the dovecote," Coo said, picking the large globs of dust from the vacuum bristles off Roohoo's feathers. "He wants to live with you."

"Absolutely not!" Tully looked up from the table, where she was paying bills. "Milton Burr can stay forever, but this one—out! Tomorrow, if he doesn't stop breaking things. You tell him that."

"Hrmph," Roohoo said when Coo translated, and for good measure he tugged the auto-retracting vacuum cord with his beak so it whipped back into the machine, spooking both Coo and Tully.

As the days passed, Roohoo and Burr hardly spoke, except to exchange grumbling criticisms of each other.

"Too nice to humans, you," Roohoo spat as he waddled by Burr helping Tully line up her spice jars in a neat row.

"Hyper as a squab, you," Burr huffed as Roohoo rode up and down Tully's window shade, hanging on by his beak.

"Eat like a human, you," Roohoo said, watching Burr daintily nibble pancakes from his own small dish.

Roohoo didn't believe in eating from dishes—not his own at least. Ignoring the plates Coo set out for him, he snatched whole pieces of bread from the toaster, dive-bombed salads, and at dinner one night retreated to the top of the refrigerator with three ravioli from Tully's bowl. He left the small plate that Coo had prepared for him untouched.

"This bird has no manners," Tully said, chasing

him with a spatula. "Tell him to go eat his own ravioli."

Roohoo kicked a roll of paper towels from the fridge onto Tully's head.

"Enough!" Tully growled.

Coo tried to make Roohoo understand about food, about how humans divided it into portions and ate slowly, and about how rude it was to take food that was someone else's. But the point of politeness was lost on Roohoo.

"Belongs to no one, food," he said, nipping a ravioli from Coo's bowl. "Until you swallow it. Silly humans."

Spending time with Roohoo made Coo appreciate Burr more than she ever had before. Pigeons cared more about the flock than about each bird in it, but they were still individuals. Coo thought that Burr, in his quiet way, was the most individual of all. What other bird would have gone the lengths he did to rescue and raise her? Burr was the reason she was Coo.

~ ~ ~

"Who is this new bird? He isn't like Milton Burr," Aggie said when she finally came down for a visit.

Roohoo had figured out how to turn on the ceiling fan. He was riding on one of the blades and hooting.

"His name is Roohoo," said Coo.

Roohoo noticed Aggie and dropped down from the fan and onto Coo's head.

"Face windows, human," he murmured, peering at Aggie eyes. "Always curious about them, me."

Before Coo could stop him, he snatched Aggie's glasses. Aggie screeched. Roohoo flew to the top of the bookshelf.

"Roohoo, no!" Coo yelled in pigeon. "Give them back, you!"

"Silly pigeon, you," Burr said, hobbling back and forth on the sofa.

Tully burst out from her room, where she'd been on the phone again.

"What is happening?" She looked from Aggie, who was crying, to Coo, to Burr.

Coo pointed to the bookcase, where Roohoo perched with one blue arm of Aggie's glasses in his beak.

"You're lucky I'm a vegetarian or you'd be pigeon pie tonight!" Tully yelled. Scooping Burr out of the way, she jumped onto the sofa and reached for Roohoo, who promptly dropped Aggie's glasses and flew to the top of the refrigerator.

"Come down right now," said Tully, grabbing a broom. She began poking the handle around the cereal boxes. Roohoo ran back and forth and kicked two boxes onto her head. Cornflakes scattered everywhere. "You're going in the cage, and not just when you need to use the bathroom!" At least Roohoo had been as quick as Burr to learn that part of living at Tully's house.

Roohoo dashed across the table, knocking an open jug of orange juice onto the floor, then fled to the ceiling fan.

Coo fetched Aggie's glasses for her.

"I'm sorry," Coo said. "Not broken."

"Thanks." Aggie wiped her eyes before putting them back on. "I don't think I like this bird."

"What a mess!" said Tully, looking at the soup of cornflakes and orange juice. She put down the broom. "We don't have enough paper towels for this. I'll run to the corner store. Girls, don't let him set fire to the apartment while I'm gone." She glared up at Roohoo, and he glared back.

As soon as the door shut behind Tully, Aggie turned to Coo.

"Okay, what's going on? Why is this pigeon— what's his name?"

"Roohoo."

"Why is Roohoo here? He doesn't look injured. And *who* was that lady who showed up after we were at the park last Saturday?" Aggie adjusted her glasses with both hands. "Tell me! Fast, before Tully gets back."

"Lucia," Coo said. "Lucia who used to be a

social worker and thinks Tully is doing everything wrong so I might be taken away." The words came quickly. Maybe Tully's insistence that she talk all the time was helping. "Roohoo is here because those guys from the city tried to kill my flock. They poisoned them."

"Hold on, *what*?"

Coo managed to explain everything that had happened with Lucia, the pigeons, and Roohoo, and told her the terrible news from Nicolas about the other flocks.

"But your flock is okay?" Aggie asked when Coo was done. "Tully's veterinarian gave them medicine and everything?"

"Yeah," said Coo. "They're getting better."

Roohoo dove down from the ceiling fan and started to peck at the juice-soaked cornflakes on the floor, but Burr hopped over from the table and chased him away.

"Are the pigeons going to come live here when they get well?" said Aggie. "All of them?"

Coo tried to picture it in more detail than she had before. Tully's apartment was bigger than the dovecote, and it had lots of food that pigeons liked, but it already felt very crowded with just a second bird. She couldn't imagine most of the flock would be happy cooped up all day, either. And Tully would be even less happy about it after the Roohoo experience.

"No, I don't think so," said Coo.

"But what if those bad guys come back?" Aggie sank down into one of the kitchen chairs, carefully avoiding the orange juice. She nudged at her glasses and frowned. "They could hurt them again. Even if they went to a different roof."

Memories of her flock lying sick and helpless in the alley, not even able to fly, flashed through Coo's mind. She pictured lots of pigeons—flock after flock—sick and dying in the same way. She felt dizzy.

"Need to help them," Coo said. "Need to leave. All pigeons in the city."

Before Lucia or people like her take me away, she wanted to add, but Aggie spoke first.

"I guess pigeons leaving the city is one way to do it," Aggie said thoughtfully. "But where would they go?"

"The woods? North?" said Coo.

"I went there once on a field trip," Aggie said. "There were lots of trees. Kids on the other bus saw a bear. I don't remember seeing any pigeons, though."

"I will go with the pigeons," Coo said. "Tully, too."

"You?"Aggie said after a pause. "Go away?"

Coo was shocked to see Aggie's lip trembling. She wasn't sure, but it looked like Aggie was about to cry.

"For how long?" Aggie asked in a very quiet voice.

"Until the pigeons are safe. Maybe quick." Truthfully, Coo wasn't sure how long that would be. Maybe forever, she thought, but she didn't want to tell Aggie that.

"How will you get there?" asked Aggie.

"Um, flying."

"Like by plane?"

"No. By pigeon."

Aggie's eyes went wide. "With Tully, too?" she said. "It sounds scary."

"I have to help the pigeons."

"I know they need help, it's just . . ." Aggie frowned, then lifted up her glasses and rubbed her eyes. They were wet again. "Everything has been so much better since I met you. I don't want you to go away."

Coo felt tears come to her own eyes.

"But we can secretly visit each other," Aggie continued, taking a deep breath. "And send messages by pigeon! I know about pigeons who carried messages on their ankles during World War Two. They saved people. Maybe some from your flock could do that? They could come to my fire escape."

"I guess so." Coo thought of New Tiktik, who was always so helpful. "Yes."

"I wish you were going to be here for Lunar New Year. It's this month. My family does all kinds of things to celebrate. My dad even cooks."

Coo felt a sudden sharp longing mixed with fear. There would be no holidays in the woods. She looked at Queenie, smiling on the loveseat. Would there be enough room to bring both Burr and Queenie, and all the food and supplies she'd need?

"I wish I had a pet horse," Aggie continued. She stared dreamily at the window. "I would lend him to you and Tully so you could run away more easily. Or I could ride him to visit you, or something."

"Thanks," Coo said, swallowing. She felt sick.

The door opened, and Aggie quickly grabbed Coo's pinky in hers.

"Don't worry, Coo. We'll be friends forever. No matter where we are."

Chapter Twenty-Three
Bread, Peanut Butter, and Flowery Shampoo

The evening after Aggie left, Nicolas called to say the flock was well enough to be released. In the morning he would drive them home in his taxi. Tully told Coo that she and Nicolas had discussed trying to find some new place nearby for the flock to live, but thought they would just return to the roof and dovecote on their own anyway. Pigeons nearly always returned to where they were born, no matter how far away. But the woods would be so peaceful and safe, Coo was sure for once the birds would decide to stay put. Other things worried her more.

"Is Lucia going to come back?" Coo sat at the table in her pajamas with her before-bed snack of graham crackers and milk.

Burr sat on her lap pecking at crumbs. Roohoo watched silently from the top of the fridge.

Tully chewed her own graham cracker and swallowed slowly. "Why are you worrying about Lucia? She called me with some ideas of how to help. They might work."

"But how do you know?"

"Earlier this week Lucia spoke to a lawyer at her old office," Tully said quietly. "She says—she says it will be a tough case, but it's possible we can stay together."

Possible? Coo knew *possible* and *definitely* meant two very different things.

"We can leave the city." Coo's voice trembled. "Fly away with my flock to the woods. Then they will be safe, too. No police. No Lucia."

Tully slowly shook her head.

"Lucia doesn't want to hurt either of us, Coo."

"How do you know? We have to help the pigeons. We can fly!"

At the sound of Coo's raised voice, Burr hopped onto the table. Tully got out a whole graham cracker for him.

"No, Coo. We don't have anywhere to go right now, or any way to get there." It was as if Tully hadn't heard her. "It's expensive to start over somewhere new. I would need to save up money for a new apartment. We would have to lie and hide, and that never ends well."

"We will live in the woods. No other people."

"That would be nice someday, Coo, but it takes planning."

"We can plan and go tomorrow." Coo stood up and looked around the apartment.

"Sit down and finish your snack, please," said Tully. "Planning takes a long time."

"What if Lucia takes me away first?" Coo sat back down.

"Coo, you are misunderstanding the situation." Tully looked at her. "Lucia isn't going to come take you away, okay? She's my friend, and she wants to help us."

"Then why does she scare you?"

Tully raised her eyebrows. "Not much gets past you, does it? You're right; she does make me nervous. But only because I've done everything wrong, and kept you a secret, and she knows. Now I have to trust her to keep you a secret. Or to help me." Tully sighed. "Hopefully both."

The bite of graham cracker in Coo's mouth became huge and tasteless as cardboard. She spat it out.

"We have to leave right now, Tully! We can go back to the roof. You can live with me on the roof. Then we help the flocks."

Coo stood up again. Her mind was racing.

"No, Coo. Neither of us can go live in the woods. Or the roof."

"Wrong." Coo stamped her foot. "Get away from Lucia. Quick."

"Coo, it's not just Lucia. We are going to have to deal with Lucia or someone like her at some point." Tully put her head in her hands. "And there are so many unanswered questions bothering me. What if your real family is out there looking for you? I've checked, but how do we know for sure? What if someone is looking for you, and it's my fault they never find you? That would break my heart."

Coo stared at Tully, baffled. Tully knew her story. She was abandoned, and the pigeons had saved her. No one else wanted her. Why would Tully question it? Didn't she believe what Coo told her?

"You are my real family. You and Burr and the flock."

"Yes, we're family. I don't ever want to go back to life without you. But something has to change. There is no way for me to keep you a secret and also give you a stable, normal life, with school and proper care."

"No school. Just you and me and Burr always, like now."

"But Coo, I worry about things like—well, what if something happened to me?"

"*Happened* to you?"

"What if I died? I know it's scary, but—"

"You can't die," Coo said confidently. "Ever."

Tully smiled. "That's news for modern science. But I have to think about what would happen to you if I did, or if I became sick."

"I will live on the roof." Coo said it automatically, even though her heart sank as she thought about it. Life alone with the pigeons wasn't enough anymore. Too much had changed.

"Not an option, Coo."

"You will not die, Tully."

"Not for a very long time, I hope." Tully pulled Coo into a hug. "The most important thing is this. No matter what, know that I love you and I will do everything I can to make sure you're safe. Always.'"

Coo wrenched herself out of Tully's arms.

"No!" she shouted. "Not the most import-ant thing. Most important thing is that we are all together. You, me, and Burr! And pigeons are safe!"

In the midst of Coo's outburst, Roohoo swept down to the table and carted the whole box of graham crackers up to the top of the fridge. No one tried to stop him.

"Humans have laws, Coo," Tully said in a very tired voice. "I'm not the kind of person who can get away with breaking them."

Coo shut her eyes. The flock laying sick in the alley. The pictures of Nicolas's far away family. Cars hurting people and animals. So much was wrong with the way humans did things.

"I hate humans! I hate them!"

Coo's fear turned to anger. She felt it rise up and froth in her like a pot of noodles boiling over. She clenched her hands into fists. Human language was suddenly too hard. She dove into her nest and buried her head in the newspaper and blankets. She shut her eyes so tightly tiny lights burst in the darkness. She pushed away thoughts of Aggie and Tully. Instead, she burned with fury for dead pigeons and cruel human rules.

"Coo."

At the sound of Tully's voice, Coo threw her hands over her ears. When Tully touched her shoulder, she wiggled away.

"Okay, you?" Burr's wings brushed her head. "Upset, you?"

"Humans, Burr," she heard Roohoo say. "Loud, them. Can't help it. Like seagulls."

"Run away, flock," Coo whispered to Burr. "Run away, me. Soon!"

"Sleep, you," Burr said, gently pecking at her hair. "Tired, you. Sleep now."

Eyes shut, Coo felt herself began to drift off.

Much later, she woke briefly as gentle hands tucked a blanket around her and shut off the lights.

~ ~ ~

Crash. Hiss.

Something huge and small at once had made a sound like a clap of thunder and a toss of hail. But indoors.

Coo sat up. It was still dark. Burr squawked and hopped just above her.

The lights came on. Too bright.

Coo blinked and squinted.

"This dratted bird!" Tully stood in the doorway to her bedroom. "Enough!"

Scattered on the floor from the kitchen all the way into the living room were hundreds and hundreds of tiny brown pebbles. Coo realized they were dried pinto beans.

Sitting in the middle of the floor, torn plastic bag still stuck in his beak, was Roohoo.

"Can't eat rocks, you," muttered Burr. "Silly bird."

"Look like jelly beans," Roohoo sniffed. He had recently discovered candy.

Tully shuffled into the room and stared at the mess. She sat down heavily on the loveseat and rubbed her eyes. "This will take a long time to clean up."

Coo scrambled out of her nest and over to Tully. "Help you, me." Still bleary, she spoke in pigeon.

"Someday I really want you to teach me to speak pigeon, Coo," Tully said, smiling. "I often forget just how amazing it is that you can talk to birds."

"I will clean up, I mean." Shaking off the last bits of sleep, Coo began picking up the little beans.

"Coo! No. We'll do it in the morning."

Coo looked up.

"Easier without me," Coo said. "For you."

"What?"

"No me—no problems. No worrying, for you."

The thought was new but made perfect sense. All Coo had brought Tully was trouble, including Roohoo. Tully was better off without her.

"Coo, no! You have made my life so much better. Don't you understand?"

"No. I'm a problem."

Tully's eyes were damp. She opened her arms.

"Coo, stop. I love you. We will find a way to stay together. I promise, okay? I will fight to keep you with every ounce of energy in my body, and I will never mind doing so. I will always keep you safe."

Coo stepped back, shaking her head.

"Come here, sweetie," Tully beckoned. "Please don't ever think you're a problem."

Coo crawled onto Tully's lap. Snuggled there, she felt the warmth of spring sunshine and fresh pancakes. She smelled Tully's smells: bread, peanut butter, flowery shampoo. She breathed it in.

For a moment, she believed everything—even her flock—would be okay.

Chapter Twenty-Four
The Taxi Ride

Friday morning. Coo and Tully left the apartment just after six thirty. The sky was the soft, dark, peach color of the sweater Tully was knitting for Coo. The air felt warm and gentle, even though it was still winter. There was a hint of spring in the way the breeze smelled.

Coo wished it were storming. They were releasing the pigeons into—what? Everything was about as clear as a puddle. A poisonous puddle.

Would the two men come back to hurt the

pigeons in some new way? What about all the other flocks in the city? What was going to happen to her? So many troubles to solve. The lovely weather felt like a cruel joke.

The streets were mostly deserted. Tully seemed nervous. She insisted Coo hold her hand and kept looking every which way over her shoulder, especially as they got closer to the alley.

At least Coo had Burr. She peeked down the zippered front of her coat. He popped his head out and scrambled onto her shoulder.

When they reached the alley, the gate was still wide open. Tully hurried them toward the hut. The alley was deep in shadow and very cold. Coo felt goosebumps.

Roohoo was perched on the fence near the fire escape, preening his feathers. He had insisted on flying. He looked up at them briefly, then went back to grooming himself.

Coo glanced down as

she walked, then gasped. Poisoned seed was scattered in the gravel. Somehow she thought it would have vanished, but it was still there, glinting.

Tully had brought a small broom and a plastic bag with her, and while Coo watched—Tully wouldn't let her help—she scraped up all of the seed the poisoners had scattered. It took a while.

"Good riddance," Tully muttered when she was done. She tied the bag shut. "I'll find a safe place to throw this out later. Now, a snack for us."

Coo didn't have much of an appetite, but she pulled out the bag of day-old donuts from Holy Doughnuts, a fancy new shop nearby, that Tully had given her to carry. She halfheartedly munched on a blackberry-frosted cruller. Tully ate a cinnamon-dusted cake donut.

"I still miss Donut Time," Tully sighed. "They were so much better than this spot, honestly. They were no frills, but they'd been in business for decades."

Roohoo swooped over and nicked at the bag

with his beak, trying to drag it away from Coo as he flapped his wings furiously. Coo gave him a chunk of her cruller, and he flew off to eat on top of the hut. She let Burr nibble from a little strawberry jelly bombolone.

They waited.

Trains rang on the tracks. The sun rose higher until the sky above was pale yellow, then white, then blue.

Sunlight was just beginning to reach the alley when there came the sound of tires on the gravel.

They held their breath as Nicolas's yellow taxi came into view.

Nicolas popped out of the front seat, beaming, as soon as he parked. "The flock knows they're home. They sound so happy."

Suddenly all of Coo's worries left her.

The flock. Her flock. They were here, they were healed, and they were about to fly again.

Couldn't *everything* go back to normal?

She thought about her plan to fly with the flock

somewhere wild and safe. Now that she was in the alley, looking up at the roof, it seemed impossible and silly. Maybe the poisoners would never come back. Maybe no one would ever question her life with Tully, and she could try to do more chores to make up for all the headaches she'd brought into Tully's life. Maybe Lucia really would help, and nothing had to change. Maybe she could even go to Aggie's school and do homework and have a normal human life.

Maybe.

Bracing Burr with one hand on her shoulder, Coo hurried to the taxi. She opened the door and saw the stacks of cages braced with blankets. The voices of her flock rose up in a wonderful chorus.

"Home, us!"

"Roof, here!"

"Must be! Get out how, us?"

"Humans here."

New Tiktik, Old Tiktik, Hoop, and Ka. Hem and Pook and Loop. Chik and Liloo, and all of the others. Their voices were jumbled together, but Coo knew each one.

"Here, me!" Coo said.

"Coo! Coo! Coo!" the pigeons sang. Coo had never heard them sound so joyful.

"Healthy, you!" said Burr, leaning forward. "Safe, flock! Relieved, me."

Tully gently tugged Coo aside. Nicolas leaned in and began passing the plastic cages out of the car one by one. Together, Coo and Tully set them down in rows on the gravel. Roohoo landed on the edge of the taxi's roof and leaned over to watch.

"Okay," said Nicolas. "We're ready."

He showed Coo and Tully how to open the cages.

Coo's fingers shook as she pressed each latch until the doors popped. One by one, her flock mates hopped out.

"Home!" said New Tiktik. She lifted her wings and rose into the air. "Home, us!"

Coo felt her eyes fill with tears.

Soon the whole flock was swooping through the alley and high up above the roof, the rail yard, and beyond. They arced and banked and turned, their feathers shining in the morning light. Roohoo took off and joined them.

Only Burr remained, hopping gleefully on Coo's shoulder. With a sudden sinking feeling, Coo wondered how he felt. He'd never fly again. Did he miss it?

The old deep wish in Coo's bones shifted and came awake. She reconsidered her plan. If she could fly—with the flock's help—then Burr could, too. Right on her shoulder or in the pouch in her jacket.

Coo watched the pigeons and shivered.

They had just finished packing the last empty cage back into the car when a familiar white van came skidding down the alley. It jerked to a stop next to Nicolas's taxi. Stan jumped out, followed by Frank. The flock, which had settled around the alley again, took off in a panicked flight toward the old dovecote.

"Oh, no. Oh, no, no, no." Tully's eyes went wide. "Not these two. Not now! We have to get out of here. Coo, get in the taxi, quick!"

But Coo was already dashed toward the men. "*You!*" she screeched, bundling Burr into the safety of her coat as she ran. "You hurt my flock!"

Before Tully or Nicolas could stop her, Coo threw herself at Stan, who leaped back. Frank stared, slack-jawed.

"This kid is out of control," shouted Stan. "Grab her, Frank!"

Before he could, Nicolas swooped Coo up around the waist and shoved her into his taxi. Coo scrambled between the empty cages, cradling Burr with one hand. Tully jumped in after her and slammed the door. Nicolas dove into the driver's seat and started the engine, while Tully tried to buckle Coo's seat belt into place.

"Messing with city business is a criminal

offense, got it?" Stan banged on the taxi window. "We're not going to let a bunch of animal-rights nut jobs like you get away with it!"

Coo stared up at Stan's waxy, scowling face. Her heart pounded so hard, she was sure it would come right of her body. The seat belt strap dug into her neck. Her hands went to her coat, where Burr shifted nervously. Nicolas started to back the car up, but Stan refused to move. He hammered on the back windshield and tugged at the doors. Then he pulled out a phone and began snapping pictures. Tully threw her coat over Coo's head. Everything went dark.

"The cops will be here pronto!" Coo heard Stan shout. "They're going to get you people! I know you sabotaged this site."

Coo clawed at Tully's coat until she could see. Nicolas managed to maneuver the taxi past the van, where Frank paced back and forth looking bewildered, and up the alley. Coo was startled to glimpse Roohoo for a moment. He sat alone on the fence, watching. The taxi turned past the bend. Stan followed, waving his fist, then he spun around and was gone. Nicolas pulled out onto the street.

"What's going to happen to the flock, Tully?" Coo asked as Nicolas zoomed down the block and into traffic. The empty cages rattled and shifted around her in the backseat.

"A better question is what's going to happen to *us*?" Tully squinted out the back window. "I can't believe it. I see their van! They're following us! Nicolas, can you lose them?"

Nicolas turned and twisted through the streets. Coo gripped the seat and tried not to throw up. Burr popped his head out of her coat, looking just as queasy.

Nicolas kept glancing into his rearview mirror. Coo noticed his neck was wet with sweat, even though it was very cold in the car. "I'm praying that man was just bluffing," said Nicolas. "He took a photo of my taxi."

"Oh my goodness! What a mess I've made for all of us!" Tully put her head in her hands. "I am so sorry to have gotten you mixed up in this, Nicolas. If anyone asks, I'll tell them we just hailed you on the street. I promise, I'll make sure you won't be blamed."

"Stop apologizing, Tully." Nicolas waved one hand in the air. "I signed up for this. Of course I worry for myself. But who is worrying for the pigeons, if not us? Everything will be fine. Look, I don't even see the van behind us anymore, do you?"

Coo turned around. The van was gone.

Nicolas drove down streets of red-brick buildings and spindly bare trees that were almost, but not quite, the same as the ones on Tully's own block. The city was huge, much bigger than Coo pictured it in her mind. Did it just go on and on and on? How far away, exactly, were forests and places without people?

She pressed her face to the cold window. People

hurried along the sidewalks, bundled up against the wind. Did any of them think about pigeons? Did any of them care?

Nicolas turned left, and Food Bazaar's parking lot suddenly appeared. Coo realized they had been driving in circles.

"I think it's safe to go home now, Nicolas." Tully peered through the car windows, then closed her eyes. "As safe as it will ever be, at least."

Chapter Twenty-Five
Escape

Nicolas turned down Tully's street. It had reached the time of morning when the city really woke up, when kids left for school and people went out for their coffees, donuts, and bagels before work. The sidewalks were starting to bustle. Garbage trucks were out, too. Nicolas's taxi got stuck behind one.

"Thank you for everything, Nicolas," Tully said. "It's probably better if we just get out here.

Again, I am so sorry for all of this. I really can't thank you enough."

"Stop apologizing. Let's talk tomorrow," said Nicolas, leaning out of the window. "I need to come back in a few days to check the flock, make sure they're okay."

"Good-bye, Nicolas!" said Coo. "Thank you!"

The garbage truck pulled away, followed by Nicolas's taxi. Coo and Tully squeezed between some parked cars and stepped over an empty flower bed to the sidewalk.

"What a morning," sighed Tully. "I need a nap. And some more donuts."

There was a crowd on the steps of Tully's building. Coo blinked, then gasped.

Lucia and two men dressed all in blue with glinting metal gadgets on their belts and hats and in their hands stood by the stoop. Beside them was a woman in a heavy tan coat and plaid scarf.

"Lucia?" said Tully. She had turned ashen. "What are you doing here? Why are the police here?"

"Don't be alarmed!" Lucia began walking toward them, her hands out. "Tully, I have no idea. I didn't call them! They say they're looking for you. I just came by with Camille to talk to you and maybe have some coffee. We called, but you didn't answer."

"I'm an attorney," said Camille, the woman in the plaid scarf, turning to the police. "Why do you want to speak with Ms. Tully?"

"Interfering with health department business," said one of the cops. "We got a complaint. You're Bettina Tully, ma'am?" He looked at Tully, then at Coo, "We have a few questions."

Tully stood in silence on the sidewalk. If Coo had been a bird, she would have soared up to the sky for safety. But she was human, so her legs turned to jelly.

"What kind of questions?" said Lucia. She took a few steps closer, until she was standing between Coo and Tully. "Tully, you don't have to answer any questions."

"It's okay, Lucia," said Tully, her voice hoarse. "I know what this is—"

"No, Tully!" Coo couldn't fly, but she could run. Even with jelly legs. "Come on! The flock will help us! Run!"

Tully stood frozen. Coo's eyes locked with hers.

"Come *on*, Tully." Tears came, and Coo swallowed them back so her throat burned. "Not safe here, you. Because of me. I'm sorry! Please, run!"

"Honey—no." Tully shook her head. "This is not your fault. This is more complicated than—"

"Tully, please!"

"Coo! What is happening?" Aggie appeared on the apartment steps, her big pink backpack hanging off her shoulder. Beside her stood her dad.

"Not the police," Aggie gasped. "Coo, *run*!"

Tully and Lucia reached for Coo at the same time. Shielding Burr with her hands, she ducked between them and around the police. Then she bolted into the street.

Never before had she run so hard or so fast.

Voices shouted behind her, but she didn't stop. She dodged three overflowing trash cans; a man walking four Lhasa apsos on leashes; an elderly can collector balancing two huge bags on a pole over her tiny shoulders; a delivery truck sitting outside the bodega with its lights blinking and a man hauling big cartons of soda off the back; and all the terrifying morning rush-hour traffic by Food Bazaar.

Any moment she expected big police hands to yank her back.

None did.

So she kept running.

She thought about what was probably happening to Tully and gulped back tears. No matter what Tully had said before, it was clear now. Coo had brought nothing but trouble into Tully's life.

When she made it to the alley, she slowed. Despite the winter air, sweat poured off her. Her insides felt shattered. What was the point of doing anything?

Burr shifted in his pouch.

Burr.

Did you get to keep your pigeon when social workers and police took you away?

A chill ran down Coo's spine.

She knew what life was like without Tully. But without Burr? Unthinkable.

She sprinted down the alley, shot through the fence, and scrambled up the stairs to the roof.

"Here, me and Burr!" Panting, Coo plopped down by the dovecote. "Need help, me and Burr! Fast!"

Burr shimmied out of his pouch and onto her shoulder.

The pigeons gathered around, peering at them curiously. In the bright winter sun, their feathers glinted in every iridescent shade of purple, white, silver, and black, like a flock of wizards in shimmering robes.

"Sick, you?" tittered New Tiktik. "Need water, you?"

"Not sick, me. In danger, me. And pigeons, too!"

It was hard, but Coo did her best to explain everything, including the return of Frank and Stan. Every pigeon in the city was at risk.

The pigeons were baffled by her attempts to describe the woods. "All trees! Far north!" Coo said, waving her arms around. "No humans! No poison!"

"Trees? Pigeons?" Hoop asked. "Roofs, better."

There wasn't time for Coo to explain. She stood up.

"Fly there, now. Bring other flocks. Hurry!"

"Fly? You?" Ka looked at her blankly. "How?"

"Holding me, you." Coo tugged her coat. "With beaks, you. Fly to safety, us!"

"Like when she was small," piped up Burr. "Flew her then, us."

The pigeons stared at Burr, at his sling.

"Light as bread then, you," Old Tiktik said quietly. "Too heavy now, Coo."

The tears came hot and fast.

"Try, you!"

"Remember, flock. Saved us, Coo did," said Hem. "From poison. Help her, us."

Coo heard tires on the gravel in the alley below. All at once, with a realization that felt like a sudden punch, she remembered that Queenie was back at Tully's apartment. Would she ever see Queenie again? She gasped, sobbing.

Roohoo flew from the top of the dovecote and landed hard on the ground in front of Coo.

"Fly her, flock," he said. "Must try, us. Right, she is."

Coo was so shocked she stopped crying.

Roohoo was helping her?

"More clever than they seem, humans," he continued. "Clever, too, us. Fly Coo, us. Now!"

As Roohoo barked orders, there came the sound of car doors slamming and people calling Coo's name in the alley below.

"Hurry!" said Burr. "Pouch now, Coo."

Hands trembling, Coo bundled Burr back into her coat. There was hardly time to think about what they were about to do. Her stomach rumbled. No donuts in the woods. Berries, maybe? She could eat roots and nuts too, like Rapunzel after she escaped the witch's tower.

"Coo!" Tully's voice rang clearly from below. "Are you up there? It's okay! Lucia and her friend are helping us. Please don't be scared! I'm coming up to the roof!"

Beaks hooked into the fabric around Coo's hood, arms, and back. Wings beat against her and filled the air. Pigeons swooped around her in tight arcs.

"Lift!" called Roohoo, zooming from bird to bird, directing them. "Lift now!"

One, two, three.

Her coat tugged tight against her body. Never had Coo felt her own featherless heaviness so intensely. She peered down at Burr. He was calm and silent.

Four, five, six.

"Lift!" said Roohoo. "Up, all! Up!"

With a sudden lurch, Coo's feet left the ground. Between her and the roof was a foot of air. Then more. And more. The pigeons wobbled over the edge of the roof, north, over the alley and toward the rail yards.

Coo gasped. She was flying.

"Slow enough to be hawk's food, you!" Old Tiktik cried to the flock, swooping nearby. "Faster!"

The flock heaved up and pitched down. They banked to the left and then dragged to the right. Two pigeons let go and Coo plunged ten feet in an instant. Her stomach flipped and flopped. Try as they might, it seemed the flock could not speed up.

Until New Tiktik grabbed a section of Coo's hood and pumped her wings. The flock stabilized.

"Look!" shouted a voice Coo didn't recognize. "Those birds are carrying the girl!"

Someone in the alley below had seen them.

The door on the roof burst open.

"Oh my God!" Tully screamed. "Coo, *no*! Come down! Please, no!" From the corner of her eye, Coo saw Tully running across the roof. But Coo was already heading for the rail yard.

"Coo is *flying*!" Coo heard Aggie shriek from somewhere. "Daddy, look! She's going to save the pigeons!"

It was glorious. The wind whipped past her legs. She glanced down. People were running back and forth. Very tiny people. She flinched, thinking how worried Tully probably was. But then she looked up.

She was *flying*.

The flock followed Roohoo's lead, sailing over the cluttered brown rail yards and silver-black-gray roofs toward the big river. Sometimes Coo looked down and saw people jumping, shouting, and pointing, and ambulances and fire trucks with flashing red lights that seemed to be following her. But she was so high up now that she could barely hear any of it.

The sky was much quieter than she'd expected. All around her, she was bathed in its clear, bright, cold light.

Unfamiliar pigeons swooped up and pestered Coo's flock with questions, curious to know what was happening.

"Going north, us," New Tiktik told them. "Poisoned, us. Survived. Going to safety now."

"Tell other flocks, you!" Coo shouted. "All the flocks, heading north! Leading you, me! To safety!"

Many other pigeons had heard rumor of poisonings, too, and decided to join Coo's flock. Soon more pigeons arrived. And more and more.

Coo's view became dense with birds. She stared around in astonishment, her heart swelling as each new group appeared. At this rate, maybe there would soon be no more pigeons for the city to poison.

A shiver ran down Coo's spine.

Maybe she *could* save all the birds.

A broad flat ribbon of brown appeared below, dotted with different shapes rippling very slowly across its surface.

"Boats!" Coo exclaimed in English. "It's the river!"

The river was much wider than she'd imagined, much bigger than a puddle or Tully's bathtub.

Her flock didn't seem to notice. Surrounded by more and more pigeons, they swooped onward. The last roofs and streets fell away, and when Coo looked down again, she saw only the dark water far below.

She closed her eyes. Her heart was beating hard and loud in her ears. When she opened her eyes again, the water was still beneath her. The pigeons flew steadily. She started to relax, even though her neck hurt and her dangling feet were numb.

How long would it take to get to the woods?

Moments later they reached the jumble of stone and glass she'd spent so many years staring at from the roof, and her worries were swept away by awe.

Her surprise at the unexpected height and heft of the buildings was similar to how she felt the very first time she met Tully. How different things were up close! But you had to get close to find out.

"Which way, us?" called Hoop.

"North!" Coo shouted.

"North, all!" echoed Roohoo.

The flocks shifted as one, filling the spaces between the buildings until Coo could see nothing but feathers in every direction. When gaps appeared here and there, Coo was startled by the shocked human faces pressed against the skyscraper windows. Some were taking photos. Some were screaming, but Coo couldn't stop herself from giggling. She was flying!

Coo looked down in giddy wonder. City noises—sirens, horns, shouts—made a muffled rumble below, but Coo floated in a deep calm. It felt like so long ago that she'd sat at the kitchen table with Aggie, looking at Tully's palm full of sugar. Here were all those people. So many millions. Each one had a name and a family, just like pigeons. Each one had loves and hates, fears and dreams. The world was so fantastically complex and vast.

She felt Burr stir.

"Flying, me," Burr said happily, wiggling his head out of the pouch. "Feels good, air."

Coo was startled out of her daydreams by a glimpse of fields and trees, crisscrossed with lines like tangled yarn. Paths, she realized, paths that were dense with people stopping to look up.

The park!

Only a few days before, Aggie had told her about a magical thing called ice-skating. It was something you could do at the park. Coo spotted a flat white shape, almost like an egg, that people were twirling across. Was that it? It looked a lot like ballet. Aggie had talked about asking Octavia or Tully to take them ice-skating before winter was over.

"Oh well." Coo sighed. "More important, this."

They passed over more buildings, though they

were shorter, and then—Coo looked down and gasped. Below her was a churning brown ocean.

Had the pigeons gotten mixed up and flown out to sea?

No. There! Across the other river was a solid expanse of trees.

"The woods!" Coo cried with relief. "Made it, us!"

Coo was surprised to see a big bridge and some tall buildings far away, beyond the woods. But there were so many trees directly in front of her, she was sure they had reached the wild forests of the north.

"Too close, this," said Roohoo. "Can't be north."

"Know how, you?" said New Tiktik. "Left the city ever, you?"

Roohoo fell silent, and Coo was relieved.

"Getting tired, us," said Ka, letting go of Coo's pant leg. "Land now!"

"Land where, us?" asked Pook as the trees grew

larger, his beak muffled by Coo's hood. "Sleepy, me."

The pigeons had been switching off, with some of the unfamiliar flocks even helping to carry her, but all were reaching exhaustion.

"Anywhere!" said Coo. "Find a good spot, you!"

The trees were dense and brown and gray. Patchy snow soon appeared underneath them.

It was going to be cold at night, Coo realized with a sudden sinking feeling. There were no dovecotes in the woods, just like there were no dumpsters.

What if another blizzard came?

Why hadn't she thought any of this through?

"There!" Coo said shakily, pointing to a particularly dense patch of trees above a cliff.

Maybe she could build a small shelter with branches. She wished Aggie was here to help.

It was going to be hard being the only human again. But everything was up to her now—she had to try to protect the pigeons and be their leader.

"Land now!" cried Coo.

"Not north, this," muttered Roohoo, somewhere to Coo's left. "Right beside city, this." But everyone ignored him.

"Careful, all!" said Burr, peering out Coo's jacket. "Slow, all!"

But the pigeons were too tired to be careful and slow. Packed so close together and unfamiliar with judging trees, they bounced and staggered toward the ground.

Five birds lost their grip on Coo's pants, and she plunged twenty feet in two seconds.

Exhausted, more birds let go. Coo sank again, too shocked to even breathe. The tall, tangled arms of the trees were getting closer and closer. They looked like horribly spiked forks pointed straight at her.

"Crash, us!" Burr shrieked. "Jump, Coo!"

Then there were no birds holding her.

Coo wasn't flying.

She was falling.

Chapter Twenty-Six
No Dumpsters in the Woods

Coo lay blinking in a knot of branches high off the ground.

The first thing she noticed was how cold she was. Her fingers burned like she was back on the roof in a winter storm. Her cheeks were raw.

Next came the pain. Sudden and searing. Her arms, her back, her head. But worst of all was her right leg. She couldn't move it.

There were pigeons everywhere, more than she

had ever seen in one place in her life. They covered every tree and what little she could see of the ground ominously far below.

Coo was astounded. She had never dreamed so many flocks would really follow her. Thousands and thousands of birds—maybe more—were going to be safe.

"Did it, me," Coo whispered to herself.

It quickly became apparent, though, that all of those birds wanted to talk to her.

And after their long and tiring flight, they had one thing on their minds.

"Food, where?"

"Hungry, us."

"Bagels?"

"Donuts?"

"Seed?"

"Find food, you!"

"Always have food, humans!"

Some of the chattering pigeons were from her own flock, but most were not. For the first time, pigeon was a loud language. A roar filled Coo's ears.

"Quiet, all!" she pleaded. Moving her mouth hurt. "Thinking, me!"

Everything hurt. Her head felt like a cracked egg.

Where was Burr?

Hands shaking, hardly daring to breath, she tried to unzip her jacket.

"Finally!" Burr's voice rang out, muffled but bright, and Coo felt him wiggle his way toward the opening of her coat. "Stuck, me."

Burr wasn't hurt.

But Coo was.

Hurt, stuck, and hungry, too.

"Berries? Grow on bushes, them," she said weakly to New Tiktik, who sat near her head asking about the closest dumpster. Coo realized with a sudden lurch that in the wintertime, berries were probably only at the supermarket.

"No food, here," said Ka. "Your idea, Roohoo. Bad idea."

Roohoo glowered on a branch above Coo, a sullen ball of feathers.

"Thought Coo had a plan, me," he grumbled. "Wrong, me. Not so special now, Coo. And not north, this!"

"Always special, Coo is," Burr said sharply. "Saved pigeons from poison. Helped us, her. Trying her best."

"Right, Burr is," said New Tiktik. "Help us now, Coo! Food, where?"

Coo's own stomach rumbled. Her triumphant joy had rushed away like a plastic bag caught in the wind.

What in the bare winter woods could thousands of hungry pigeons and one human girl possibly eat?

"Tree bark?" Coo suggested hopefully.

"Gives stomachache, tree bark," said Ka.

"Roots?"

The pigeons looked at her blankly.

"Too scared to think earlier," Coo mumbled.

"Bad idea, this. Made a mistake, me."

Everything had happened much too fast. Back on the roof, with the police and Lucia and the poisoners all in pursuit, flying away had seemed like the only option— the best chance to save the birds and Tully, too.

But what kind of solution was this? No food, no shelter, and frigid cold.

"Hungry, me," whined Pook. "Need food *now*, me."

"Food soon," said Coo. "Find some, me. Somehow."

She tried to haul herself up and out of the branches, but the pain in her leg made it impossible to move.

"Fix it, me," Coo said, wincing. "On my way." Despite the pain, despite the way things seemed to be turning out, she had to try.

"Hurt, Coo is," Burr said. "Worried for her, me."

A murmur of anxiety rippled through the flock.

"Rest now, you," Burr said to Coo, gently pecking at her hair. "Help you, us."

"Get food after a rest, me," Coo said weakly. "Find food for all, me."

Burr crawled back into the pouch in her coat. Coo sighed. At least something was warm and familiar.

Night fell. The woods were dark, much darker than anywhere Coo had ever been before. Twigs snapped. Pigeons murmured and shuffled their wings. Instead of comforting her like they did in the dovecote, the sounds spooked Coo. She began to shiver with cold. Her eyes grew heavy. At Burr's urging, her flock covered her body as best they could, just like they always had in snowstorms.

She thought of Tully. A new ache ripped through her that felt almost as bad as her injuries. She hoped the police had let Tully go when they realized Coo had run away.

"Better off without me, her," Coo mumbled to

herself in pigeon, just before slipping into sleep. "Help the birds at least, me."

"There she is! In the tree! Those pigeons are all over her, but she's moving."

"She looks injured. Quick, tell the others! Get the EMTs!"

Voices. Human voices.

Coo tried to open her eyes. The sun was bright. She quickly shut them again. At least her leg didn't hurt anymore. She couldn't feel it at all.

She heard the sound of pigeons beating their wings and lifting into the air. Human hands grabbed her. Someone began hacking at the tree limbs around her. Slowly she felt herself being lowered to the ground.

"My name is Aviva. I'm here to help you. What's your name? Can you speak?"

Coo managed to focus on the person talking to her. A woman with large worried eyes and dark hair pulled back in a tight bun.

"We're getting you out of here, sweetie," the woman said. "Don't worry. Don't move just yet."

"No! Need to stay in the woods!" Coo gasped, using what little strength she had left. "Have to help the pigeons keep away from the poison! Far from humans! Up north!"

"Up north? Far from people?" Aviva frowned. "You're in the big nature preserve next to the city. It's just across the river." She pointed. "The wilderness in the north is hours and hours away. This is the suburbs."

Coo blinked. Nature preserve? The suburbs? She tried to sit up, but it hurt too much.

"The pigeons are in danger!" She felt Burr shift in his pouch as she shouted. "The mayor wants to hurt them all. Help them! Need to stop him!"

"Shh, try to stay calm, and stay still," said Aviva.

Coo looked down at her leg and gagged. It twisted strangely, like no leg should. She felt dizzy, even dizzier than she had been when she was at her hungriest on the roof.

"Tully," Coo whispered. Strange spots were swimming around her vision, and she shut her eyes. "Help me, Tully."

"Help is coming, sweetie." Even though Coo could feel Aviva's hands on her shoulders, the woman's voice sounded farther and farther away. "Just stay with me."

Chapter Twenty-Seven
Healing

It took a long time to sort everything out.

It started in the hospital back in the city, where Coo had to go so that the doctors could fix her leg.

"Pigeons!" she told everyone she met in her first delirious hours there. "The pigeons are in danger! The mayor is trying to kill them. We must stop the poisoning. Listen to me!"

"Hush, don't worry now," the nurses and doctors told her, if they said anything at all. Most looked at her with worry etched all over their faces, worry as intense and frightening as the endless beeps and alarms going off all around her.

"Where is Burr?" Coo asked anyone she met. "My pigeon, Burr! Where is he?"

No one answered her. She tried desperately to remember the moments after her rescue from the tree and where he had gone, but it was all a horrible blankness.

"Tully?" she asked a group of people who came into her room and talked over her head. She clawed at the strange, squeezing plastic sleeve someone had put on her upper arm. "Is Tully here? Is she okay?"

"You need to lay down and relax," a woman said as she leaned over Coo. "Everything will be fine. There's nothing to worry about."

Coo shut her eyes, her heart pounding. All of her worst fears had come true. Burr was missing, and Tully had abandoned her—or maybe she had been arrested. How would anything ever be okay again?

"I never thought pigeons could raise a kid," a nurse named Simone said as she gently changed some of Coo's bandages late one night. "Let alone fly one across the city! I couldn't believe it when I heard about you. You're something else."

"Pigeons? Pigeons are safe?" Coo reached out and gripped Simone's hand. It was hard to tell time in the hospital, but several days had passed, she guessed, and no one had answered any of her questions about the birds, much less mentioned them to her.

"Safe? Safer than they were before you came along, that's for sure."

Coo would have leaped out of bed right that moment, but her leg was stuck in a frightening mess of hard plaster and suspended above the bed in a tangle of ropes and metal sticks the nurses called traction. She could hardly move at all. "Mayor is hurting them! I need to help them! You help me?"

"Shh, dear. Don't get worked up. You don't

know anything that's going on, do you?"

In the dimly lit hospital room, Simone's face was both worried and kind. "Hold tight a moment," she said. "I'll be right back."

She returned with a box of orange juice and a small bag of cookies in one hand, and a giant stack of newspapers in the other.

"I don't know if I'm supposed to be doing this," Simone said, shuffling through the papers. "But it's ridiculous they're keeping you in the dark. Aha, here's one from yesterday. See?"

Coo recognized the newspaper, but she was shocked to see what was staring back at her from the front page.

Her own face!

Scratched, leaf littered, and dazed, but her. The photo must have been taken just after she was rescued from the tree. Gathered all around her was a blur of pigeons—hundreds and hundreds of pigeons.

"There's a whole article, too," said Simone.

"Can't read all this," said Coo, scanning the photograph, desperately looking for Burr.

"I can read it to you when I'm done with my rounds, but look." Simone pointed to the page. "Half the world saw you fly across the city. Everyone is fascinated by your story. And believe me, thanks to you everyone knows about Mayor Doherty's plan to hurt the pigeons." Simone smiled. "He's not going to get away with it."

Coo lay back on the stiff hospital pillows, stunned.

Burr was missing, her leg was broken, and Tully was obviously so angry that she wanted nothing more to do with her, since she hadn't come to the hospital even once, but maybe everything wasn't a total disaster.

Maybe she had managed to help the pigeons after all.

"You eat these cookies and drink your juice," said Simone. "And try to rest, okay? You've been through a lot. You need to heal."

Healing

The next morning a woman named Deb appeared. She was small and prim and tidy, like a young pigeon, even though the wrinkles around her eyes made Coo wonder if she was older than Tully.

"I'm here to help you, Coo," Deb said, smiling. "I'm your caseworker, okay?"

Coo's eyes widened. *Caseworker.* That word was familiar. Deb was like Lucia before she retired.

"First, let me know what you have questions about," said Deb. She pulled a pen and a big folder of papers from her tote bag.

"Where is Burr?"

Deb looked confused, so Coo tried again.

"My pigeon. He is also named Milton. Milton Burr. Where is he?" Coo held her breath. If Deb didn't know where he was, who would?

"Oh, of course!" Deb grinned. "What a kind little bird he is. I can tell you firsthand he's just fine. I met him recently. He is at Bettina Tully's apartment."

Tears burned Coo's eyes and her scratched cheeks. She leaned back against the pillows and exhaled.

"I can see you're really attached to him," Deb said softly, and made a note on her papers.

"What about my flock?" Coo asked, rubbing her eyes. "Roohoo? New Tiktik? Hoop?"

"Sorry, sweetie." Deb frowned and shook her head slightly. "I'm not familiar with those names. But Tully did tell me that the pigeons you lived with were okay."

Coo's tears of relief about Burr and the flock mixed with aching sadness about Tully. Clearly Tully was angry at her. Otherwise, why had she stayed away? Why wasn't she here with Deb?

"Do you have any questions about Tully, Coo?" asked Deb.

"She is not here," whispered Coo. She shrugged and stared at her leg until her eyes blurred.

"Well, she very much wants to adopt you," said Deb. "But it's going to take time to sort out, and you can't see her quite yet."

"She . . . she still wants me?" Coo looked up.

"Of course." Deb's eyebrows rose. "Yes, very much, Coo."

"But she is not here."

"She *can't* be here." Deb shook her head. "I know it's confusing. Until the judge reviews everything, she isn't allowed to contact you at all. I'm sorry, honey."

Coo stared at Deb.

"A lot of people want to see you two back together," said Deb. "But there's a process. We have to make sure everything is done right."

"I will live with her?" Coo swallowed. "Soon?"

Deb paused. She looked very serious. "I can't promise it just yet."

"I want to go home," Coo whispered. She could barely hold back more tears. "Right now, please."

"Soon, I hope," Deb said. She paused, then rummaged through a tote bag in her lap. "I do have some mail for you."

It was a big flat envelope with small cat stickers

all over the front. Reading still came slowly for Coo, but she recognized AGGIE in the top left corner at once. She ripped open the envelope.

Inside was a glittery card, a pack of more cat stickers, and a book called *Pippi Longstocking*. Deb helped Coo read Aggie's card:

Dear Coo,

Seeing you fly was the scariest thing ever! But it was also amazing. I'm so happy you are okay. Did falling hurt a lot? I am thinking of new dances for you with crutches. My dad did a story on the pigeons. The mayor is in trouble. I hope you like the book I got you, Pippi is brave like you.

I hope your leg and everything heals fast.

I MISS YOU.

Love,

Your friend Aggie

P.S. I have been trying to get Milton Burr to teach me pigeon. I think he says he misses you.

"Oh, and most important of all," Deb said, reaching into her bag again. "This is for you!"

"Queenie!" Coo buried her nose in her doll's yarn hair.

Queenie wasn't Tully, or Burr, but she smelled like home, and all at once Coo missed her old life with an ache that made her gasp.

"Lonely, me," she whispered to Queenie. "Want to go home, me."

Could Deb be right? Did Tully really want her back?

Coo hugged Queenie even tighter, hardly daring to hope.

Chapter Twenty-Eight
Surprise

Days passed into weeks before the doctors said Coo's leg was ready to come down from its complex tangle of pulleys and bars. It was still broken, and she still needed a cast, but she could start to move around on crutches. The nurse named Simone helped her make a little sling out of some old sheets for Queenie, who rode on her back while Coo practiced inching down the halls.

One morning soon after, Deb arrived and said, "Good news, Coo."

She stepped aside and through the doorway appeared—

Tully.

She looked exactly the same, even though everything had changed. In her hands she held a familiar pile of wool. Coo's old hat and scarf.

"I'm here to take you home, Coo," said Tully, smiling. "Finally. I've been waiting for this day for so long."

Coo blinked, too shocked to speak.

"I would have come back sooner, but they wouldn't let me in." Tully's voice broke. "I was so worried about you!"

"Thought you were mad at me," Coo said when she found her voice. "Thought you didn't want me."

"*Mad* at you? What? Coo, no." Tully's eyes filled with tears. "You're my family, and you were trying to help. I could never be mad at you for that."

"I messed up," Coo said, her voice catching.

"Ran away—flew away—caused you trouble—"

"Coo, stop. You did the only thing you knew how to do." Tully paused. "But please, never do it again!"

"You are really not mad?"

"No! I *love* you, Coo."

Tully enveloped her in a hug, a hug that smelled just like Tully, like nothing had changed, and Coo never knew she had so many tears inside herself. A whole puddle full of tears, a puddle she'd been collecting all during her time in the hospital and even before.

"We're going home." Tully was crying, too, and her words came out warbly and fast. "I love you forever, Coo. We're each other's family, and we're going home for good."

Outside the hospital, the city noises were sudden, loud, and jarring. Coo shrunk into the wheelchair the nurses had insisted Tully use to bring her down in the elevator. Coo held her crutches across her lap. It was spring now, but there was a damp, cold wind blowing through the busy street. The trees had shredded Coo's comfy red corduroy coat from Goodwill, and she missed it with a sudden pang. She wore a new puffy pink coat Deb had brought to the hospital for her. It was warm but felt unfamiliar. Keeping the crutches balanced with one elbow, she wrapped her old scarf more snugly around her neck and draped one end around Queenie.

Nurses and doctors came to say good-bye. Simone gave her a hug. Tully held Queenie and helped Coo stand up on her crutches. Coo's leg pinched and ached. She felt a flicker of begrudging gratitude for cars. And she thought of Burr. His injury must have been so much more painful than he ever let her know.

Nicolas was waiting in his taxi. He helped Tully maneuver Coo into the backseat and put her crutches in the trunk.

Coo noticed a small white cage sitting on the floor, just like the ones Nicolas had used

to transport the sick flock. Tully pulled it up from its bed of towels and opened the latch.

"Someone came along to say hello," Tully said.

Coo's heart was beating very fast. She could hardly speak.

Burr!

He hobbled right up onto her shoulder, just as though nothing had ever changed.

"Safe, you!" he said. "So worried, me."

"Sorry, me." Coo gulped back sobs. "Made such a mistake, me. Flying—woods—"

"Hush," said Burr. "Don't worry, you. Trying to do good, you."

"Went all wrong."

"Don't belong in woods, pigeons," said Burr. "Belong with people, pigeons. For good or bad. Always knew this, me. But scared, too, me."

"Pigeons safe now," Coo whispered. "No more killing. Mad at me, flock?" Coo held her breath.

"Mad?" said Burr. "No. Fun adventure, woods! Hungry. And fun."

"Happy to be going home, me," Coo said, sighing with relief. "Always care for you, me. Always! Never apart again, us."

"Home always now, you," said Burr. "You and me."

Coo cuddled Burr while they drove. The traffic made everything very slow. At a red light, Nicolas turned around and grinned at Coo. Coo blushed.

"Nothing to be shy about." Tully patted the seat beside her and Coo hesitantly, then with relief, snuggled in closer. "We're all just glad you're here. We'll be at our new apartment in no time."

"You can just talk in pigeon if you want," said Nicolas, smiling in the rearview mirror. "None of us mind. I want to learn. Nothing could be more useful to a veterinarian!"

Coo laughed and felt a little less awkward.

She held Queenie up to the window, and they watched the city stream by. So many humans walking and talking and running across the streets. Flocks of pigeons arced overhead and pecked at the paper and plastic spilling from the trash cans onto the sidewalks. She wondered if any were among the many who had traveled with her. From the corner of her eye, she was startled to see a pigeon who looked exactly like Roohoo, resting on a parking meter and staring back at her. But before she could look more closely, the light changed and the taxi took off again.

"My flock," she asked Tully, turning away from the window. "Back on the roof okay?"

"As far as we can tell," said Tully. "Nicolas and I went over and tried to count them all. Burr helped, too; he seemed to be trying to tell us no one was missing."

"The pigeons who followed you seemed to head back to the city just fine within a few days," said Nicolas. "But it was very odd until they did."

"What do you mean?" asked Coo.

"So many pigeons left. Everyone noticed," said

Nicolas. "The city felt empty. People missed the pigeons. It was all over the news! You were all over the news, too!"

Coo smiled. Burr was right—humans were more good than not.

"Coo, I should tell you something ahead of time," Tully said, breaking the happy, humming silence in the car. "I hope it's okay. Everyone insisted, and maybe I should have said no, but . . ."

"But what?"

"Oh my goodness, it's nothing bad! Just a surprise. You'll see."

Nicolas turned down a tree-lined street and slowed to a stop in front of a big, ancient-looking brick building. It was dark burgundy, with many windows and plants and vines in front. Bobbing on strong green stems in the flower beds under the windows were big cup-shaped blooms in every shade of jelly bean.

"Our new home. Forty-one—forty-two

Forty-Second Street. Funny address, right? The kind to drive a postal worker mad." Tully smiled. "It's not far from the rail yard or our old apartment. It's a quick walk to visit the flock, or Aggie."

Tully helped Burr and Coo out of the taxi. Burr hopped on Tully's shoulder, and Tully pushed Queenie into the big pocket of Coo's puffy new coat. Nicolas drove off to find a parking spot.

The street was hushed. At the end of the block stood an even bigger building with a tall fence around it. Coo leaned on her crutches and stared. She recognized it.

"That'll be your school," Tully said. "It's Aggie's school, too."

School. So much more was about to change.

The new building's lobby was much bigger than Tully's old one. The doors were dark mahogany and arched like in a castle, and once inside there were crisscrossing beams and stained glass and a black-and-white tile floor.

There was an elevator, luckily. It zoomed them

upstairs to a hallway that Coo carefully clomped down. It took her so long that Nicolas caught up to them.

"This is our apartment," Tully said in front of the door marked 5A. Coo recognized their old floral doormat. Tully opened the door, and said, "Welcome home, Coo!"

Coo peered through the doorway into a big living room.

Aggie and her brother Henry, her sister Octavia, and father Phil were there wearing party hats and holding balloons, beaming and clapping. Bright pink and gold decorations hung over a table full of snacks. Coo looked around, speechless. She saw Tully's old blue armchair and the loveseat. She saw the pictures of Ben and young Tully on the wall, and even a new picture, one of her in the hospital that Deb or someone else must have taken. She saw Burr's cage sitting on its small table. It was a bright, clean apartment, new and familiar at once.

"Coo!" Aggie shouted. "I was so worried about you!" She threw her arms around Coo. "I'm so glad you're okay and here and that we don't have to send messages by pigeon to be friends. I mean, we could still do that. But just for fun."

Coo smiled, still too overwhelmed to speak.

"I started modern dance classes," said Aggie as Tully helped Coo take off her coat and sit in the loveseat.

Tully propped Queenie up carefully beside Coo and helped Burr onto Coo's shoulder.

Aggie ran to the table and grabbed two gold party hats—one big, one tiny—and helped Coo and Burr put them on.

"And Tully says when your leg heals you can come, too, if you want?" Aggie raised her eyebrows. "It would be the best if you were there."

Coo was about to reply when she glanced over Aggie's shoulder.

Lucia.

Coo leaned back in the loveseat and gasped.

"Don't worry," Tully said hastily, seeing the fear on Coo's face. "Lucia helped us a lot."

"It's okay." Lucia smiled. She took a few slow steps toward Coo. "We don't really know each other, and I know it was probably hard to understand what was going on."

Warily, Coo glanced at Tully, who nodded encouragingly.

"I was trying to help by bringing Camille to see Tully," said Lucia. She smiled again and shook her head at the same time. "I hoped Camille would help Tully sort everything out. I didn't expect to cause—"

"Don't apologize!" Tully interrupted. "Camille was so helpful, and all's well that ends well."

Coo peered carefully at Lucia. She was wearing her cat earrings again, but somehow they made her seem friendlier now. "You didn't want the police to take me away?" asked Coo.

"Let it be known far and wide that I did *not* call

the police!" Lucia scowled. "Those awful pigeon poisoners were the ones who called them."

"They must have written down my address," Tully said. "Back when they looked at my ID. Remember?"

Coo felt a small chill run down her spine.

"Stan Mooney and Frank Beaumont," said Aggie's dad. "Mayor Doherty is claiming they went rogue and never had permission to get rid of pigeons in the first place. Stan got fired, and Frank is on unpaid leave."

"Serves them both right," said Henry.

"Yeah!" said Aggie. She picked up Queenie and sat down on the loveseat next to Coo. "Even Octavia agrees that they aren't rats with wings."

Aggie's sister leaned against the wall and crossed her arms. "I maybe, possibly, said that once, but I never thought pigeons should *die*." Octavia scrunched up her mouth and cocked her head toward Burr. "This one who lives with Tully is pretty cute."

"Yes, he is," said Aggie, and leaned over to tickle Burr under his beak.

"Lucia, you helped us so much. And you, too, Nicolas," Tully said suddenly. Her voice shook like she was almost crying. "I don't know how I'll ever be able to thank you both enough. I'm so sorry for what I put you through."

"Good grief!" said Nicolas. He laughed. "Enough of the apologies and gratitude, Tully. We're just happy Coo and the pigeons are safe."

"Exactly," said Lucia. "I'm thrilled I could help. And now I just want to eat all this delicious food!"

With that, the party got started. There was a lentil salad made by Henry, and a fresh batch of peppermint brownies baked by Octavia, and strawberry-guava cake from a bakery down the block, and music that Nicolas found on Tully's radio, and lots of stories from Aggie's dad about Coo and pigeons in the news and the reluctant way the mayor was forced to apologize about the poisoning.

Aggie and Coo performed the hawk attack scene from *Pigeon Roof*, with Coo on her crutches acting as the wounded bird. Everyone clapped.

It was starting to get late when there was a sudden *tap-tap-tap* on the window that led out to a fire escape.

"What is that?" said Aggie's father. "Are those pigeons out there?"

Coo gasped and tried to stand. "My flock! I see New Tiktik, and Hoop."

"What? How?" asked Aggie, running over to the window.

"That's your flock, Coo?" said her father. He pulled out a tiny notebook. "Here?"

"Open the window, Aggie!" Coo scrambled for her crutches and swung across the room with Burr clinging to her shoulder. More familiar pigeons crowded the fire escape. "Hurry!"

"Wait." Tully groaned, peering over Aggie's head. "Is that—is that Roohoo? It is. Oh, please, no."

Henry helped Aggie wrench the window open,

and soon Coo's flock was zooming around the room. Nothing was wrong. They were just there to join the party.

Roohoo settled on Coo's arm.

"Been following Tully for weeks, me," he said. "Human, her. Never noticed! Saw you at the big building. Followed you in the yellow car. Got the whole flock together, me. Miss you, us. Happy you're back, me."

Then he jumped into the middle of what was left of Coo's cake and took a giant nibble.